MUSTANG MAN

MUSTANG MAN
LOUIS L'AMOUR

BANTAM BOOKS
TORONTO · NEW YORK · LONDON · SYDNEY

MUSTANG MAN
A Bantam Book

PRINTING HISTORY
Bantam paperback edition / May 1966
Louis L'Amour Hardcover Collection / February 1983

If you would be interested in receiving bookends for The
Louis L'Amour Collection, please write to this address for
information:

The Louis L'Amour Collection
Bantam Books
P.O. Box 956
Hicksville, New York 11801

ISBN 0-553-06237-9

Published simultaneously in the United States and Canada

Bantam Books are published by Bantam Books, Inc. Its
trademark, consisting of the words "Bantam Books" and the
portrayal of a rooster, is Registered in U.S. Patent and
Trademark Office and in other countries. Marca Regis-
trada. Bantam Books, Inc., 666 Fifth Avenue, New York,
New York 10103.

PRINTED IN THE UNITED STATES OF AMERICA

0   9   8   7   6   5   4   3   2

MUSTANG MAN

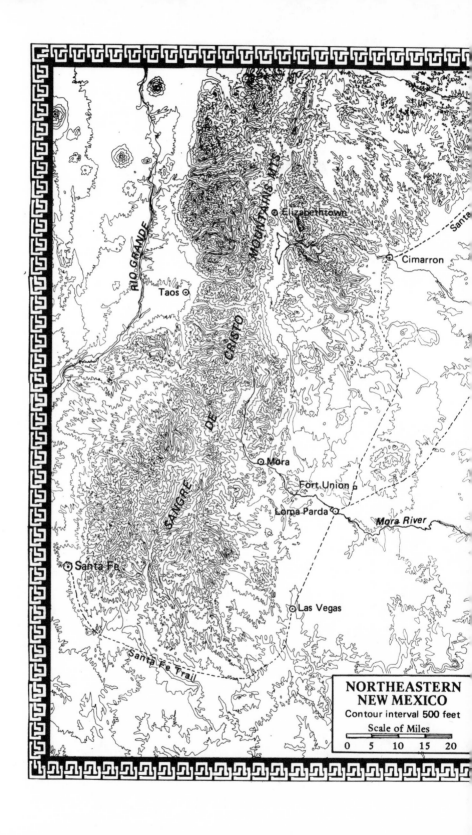

NORTHEASTERN
NEW MEXICO
Contour interval 500 feet
Scale of Miles
0   5   10   15   20

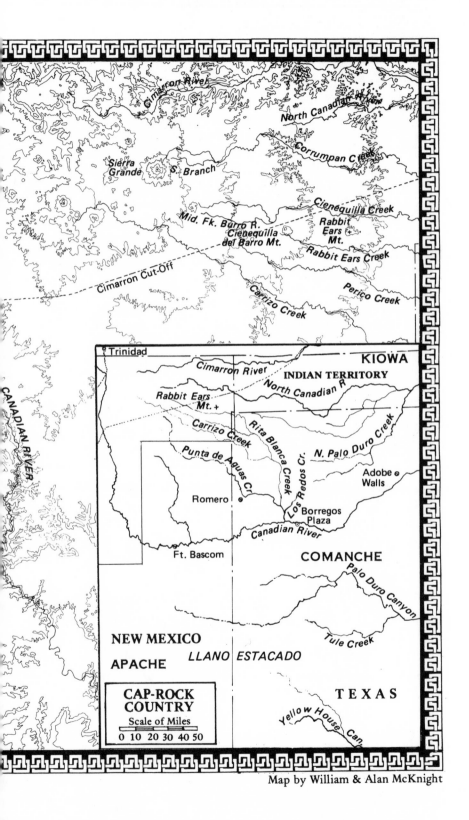

Map by William & Alan McKnight

ONE

When I came down off the cap rock riding a wind-broken bronc, half of New Mexico must have been trailin' behind me, all ready to shake out a loop for a hanging.

Nobody told me I should wait around and get my neck stretched, so when I'd seen them coming my way I just wrapped myself around the nearest horse and taken off down country. Seemed likely those boys would run out of ambition before long, but they must have been mighty shy of entertainment in that gyp-rock country, because they kept a-coming.

Me, I high-tailed it out of there as fast as that bronc would take me, and for a spell that was pretty fast. Only the bronc had run himself out trying to save my bacon and now I needed myself a fresh horse, or else I'd never need another.

About that time I sighted a clump of cottonwoods down on the flat, and cottonwoods spell water in any man's country. Water usually meant there was stock close by, and probably folks. Where there was either there might be a horse.

So right then I began building myself a fresh dust cloud behind me, and when I rode up to those trees I was just a-fogging it. Sure enough, there were horses there, and some mighty fine stock, too. So I shook out a loop and dabbed it on a handsome line-back dun with a black mane and tail.

Snubbing him to a post, I stepped down and unlatched my saddle and threw it on the dun. I cinched up tight, and was about to climb into the leather when I heard the click of a cocked hammer and froze right where I was. That gun was behind me, but judging by the sound the range was no more than twenty feet; and my ma never raised no foolish papooses. Back there in the Clinch Mountains of Tennessee we boys learned to use guns mighty early, but

1

we also learned to hold them in respect. When a man puts a gun on you, you've no cause to believe he won't use it.

"Mister"—the voice was dry and cold—"you sure ain't pa'tic'lar where you put your saddle."

"Figured I was mighty pa'tic'lar. If that ain't the best horse in the lot, you show me a better and I'll switch my saddle."

He chuckled, but I knew that rifle hadn't moved any. This was a hard man there behind me.

"What you figure gives you title to that horse?"

"You keep an eye on the rim of the cap rock yonder, and when you see dust a-fetching up over the rim you'll know what gives me title. Those boys back yonder got themselves a rope, and they figure on making me the belle of the ball."

"What did you do?"

Well, I taken a chance and turned around. That old man held a Sharps .50 buffalo gun on me, a gun that would open a hole in a man as big as your fist. He was slight built, but he had a pair of the coldest eyes you ever did see.

"I fetched my gun a mite faster'n another man; only I was a stranger, and that other man, he owned himself a big outfit and a lot of good friends."

"You got a name? Something folks call you by?"

"Nolan Sackett."

"Heard of you. Outlaw, the way folks tell it."

"Look at that rim, mister. There's your dust. Now this here ain't no time to start discussin' a man's moral outlook. There's no time to talk about my past, not if I am to have a future."

He stepped around me so's he could look at the rim, and then he said, "What d'you figure to do now, Sackett?"

"Seems to me I've got a choice between a rope and a bullet, or a rope and a chance. Folks consider me a right fast hand with a six-shooter, so I'm likely to take the chance and see if I could beat you to a killing."

"You wouldn't beat me, Sackett, but I like your sand. You get up on that horse and light out. Hold to the bottom yonder and you'll be out of sight. The canyon cuts back toward the Yellow House, and you'll have a fair run down the valley. Give that horse a spell now and again and he'll take you clear of them."

Well, I taken out. But not before I had one long look at that old man. "Thanks," I said; "and you need a friend, you call on Nolan Sackett. Or any Sackett, for that matter, for we run long on kinfolk."

That line-back dun taken out of there like he had a fire under his tail and was tryin' to outrun it. Sure enough, the canyon forked, and I went up the branch called Yellow House. An hour later, when I topped out on the cap rock again, there was no sign of pursuit. So I slowed the dun to a canter, and then to a walk.

That was wide-open country, a vast plain cut by occasional ravines, the rare streams flowing into the Arkansas or the Canadian River, although both rivers lay north of where I was riding, the Arkansas far to the north.

This was buffalo country and Indian country, and a man could lose his hair in one unwary moment anywhere within a thousand square miles. Buffalo hunters had come into it, coming out of Dodge; and here and there a few cattlemen had the idea of moving in, only mostly it was just an idea.

The outlaws had come early. Up north of the Canadian was the stretch of country they called No Man's Land, and east of there was Indian Territory. No man in his right mind rode into that country without a gun ready to hand, and the will to use it. There were canyons like the Palo Duro and the Yellow House, but mostly it was cap-rock country, and water a rare thing unless you knew where to find it.

The buffalo knew. They knew not only the few permanent springs and creeks, but rain-water lakes that sometimes lasted several weeks or even months if the rains had been heavy. Often enough, though, they vanished within a few days, so following buffalo tracks to hunt water was a chancy thing.

Nothing had ever led me to believe that anything would be easy for me. The only trails I knew were long and dusty, blazing hot or freezing cold. The nights I'd slept under a roof these past years were mighty few.

A body can get the name of outlaw sometimes without half trying, and I hadn't tried. I guess I never cared much, either. We Clinch Mountain Sacketts were good enough folk, I guess, but a mite poorer and rougher than those over in the Cumberlands or down on the flatlands.

We sprung from thin soil, and raised more kin than crops, but we were proud folk, too, and in those days a man's pride was defended by a gun. I ain't saying it was right, only that was the way it was, and gun battles were not only a matter of us feuding folks from Tennessee, nor in the West. It was the way things were done all over the country, and in Europe too, they say.

Andrew Jackson himself, him who was president of the United States, engaged in several gun battles, and killed Charles Dickinson in a duel. He got his shoulder shot up in the fight with the Bentons; and it was claimed that he had a hand in a hundred and three duels, as a fighter, a second, or a member of the party.

He was only one of many. Few prominent men avoided duels if they entered public life, where somebody might speak slander of them. Nor could a man continue to live in any community where it was known he had been called a liar and had failed to fight, or, in fact, if he had failed to fight whenever honor demanded it.

But I could lay no claim to dueling or fighting in the way of defending my honor or anybody else's. Soon as I was old enough, I drifted west, living as best I could. There was little enough at home, and when I was gone there was one less to feed. What fights I had, after the Higgins feud, were mostly with rough men who lived in the same way I did.

Now as I rode, the plains stretched wide around me, flat as a floor as far as a man could ride. Not a tree, not a bush, just the low, dusty grass, and the wide milky-blue sky above.

I took off my beat-up old hat and wiped the sweat-band. That hat had never been much account, and the bullet hole left there by a Kiowa brave before he died had done it no good.

Looking at that hat made me feel glum. A man ought to have a few worthwhile things in his life. All my years I'd honed for a store-bought suit, but I'd never managed it yet, nor even a good saddle. It was little enough a man could have unless he got lucky with cards or went west to the goldfields. Some folks had the turn for making money. Seemed to me I never did.

But that was a good horse I rode now. Maybe the best I'd ever had, and I owed that old man a debt. There was something about him I cottoned to, anyway. He was a hard old man, and he would have torn my guts out with that buffalo gun if I'd made a move for my gun; but when the chips were down and I'd been holding no more than a couple of deuces, he had come through.

Of a sudden, I saw the wagon.

For several minutes I'd been watching what looked to be a low white cloud lying off on the horizon, and hoping it was no thunderhead. Thunder storms can roll up almighty fast out there on the plains, and such lightning as you never saw. A man standing out on the level lands is a natural attraction for lightning, to say nothing of a man on horseback carrying a pistol and a rifle.

Now as I rode on I began to see it was no cloud, but a wagon top, and beside the wagon a woman was standing.

She was a mile or more off, but it was a woman, all right. What set me to fretting was that she was alone—nobody else in sight, and no stock of any kind—no horses, or mules, or oxen. And that worried me. Folks caught up with trouble out on the grasslands would do almost anything for a horse, and I was riding a good one. So I didn't just fetch up to that wagon, I veered wide around it.

That woman, she started to wave at me, but I just waved back and rode wide around her, keeping an eye on her and a hand on my rifle. Only I took time out to glance at the ground from time to time, for I wanted to know where the wagon came from, and what had happened to the horses or oxen that had hauled it there.

Horses... six head of horses heavy enough to pull that wagon, and two head of saddle horses, led off by a man afoot.

Circling on around, I came on the tracks of the wagon as it went along to the place where it now stood. The tracks had cut into the turf... that wagon was loaded, really loaded.

Right then he made a mistake, and moved. A man lying still is hard to see if his clothes blend into the background, but movement draws the eye. He was bellied down in a slight depression on the cap rock, just a-fixing to take my scalp and my horse when I came riding up.

So I pulled up a good three hundred yards off and shucked my own Winchester. Then I started circling again, and he had to keep moving to keep me in sight. By the time I'd made a complete circle he could see I'd outfoxed him, and he quit on me.

He was smart enough not to risk a bullet unless he could score a kill with the first shot, but with me moving like I was, he couldn't be sure. Even if he got a bullet into me at that distance I might ride away; or if I fell, my horse might be frightened off. Circling as I was, I could bring my rifle to bear at any moment, and I was able to make him move as I wanted.

He spoke to the woman, saying something I could not make out at that distance, and then he stood up, his hands empty. I moved in closer then, keeping them lined up ahead of me. He was surely carrying a hand-gun, and I did not like the way she was keeping one hand hidden in the folds of her skirt. Either or both of them might try a sneak shot at me. Looked to me like I'd ridden into a nest of rattlers.

At fifty yards I drew up once more, taking my time in looking them over. My rifle was held pistol-fashion in my right hand, and I was a fair shot from that position. "You shed that small gun," I told him, "and tell your woman that if she doesn't drop that pistol I'll shoot both of you."

"You'd shoot a woman?"

"If she's holding iron on me," I said, "I'd shoot her as quick as you. You tell her to drop it, mister, if you figure to watch the sunset tonight."

He unlatched his gun belt and let it fall, and that girl, she walked over to a blanket near the fire and dropped her gun. Then I rode up to them, watching like a cougar watches a rattler.

He was a slim, wiry young man, scarcely more than a boy, and he wore city clothes, but they were dusty now. He had a square, pleasant-looking, young boy's face, only when you got close enough you could see his eyes were not pleasant now.

The girl was not more than eighteen, I'd guess, and she was pretty as a white-tailed pony. And the two of them were alike as two could be.

As for me, I knew what they saw, looking at me, and it wasn't much. My jaw was blunt and my nose had been broken, and I carried most of my two hundred and fifteen pounds in my chest and shoulders. I had a fifty-inch chest above a rider's small waist, and biceps and neck that measured seventeen inches around. My fists were big and hard, the kind a man can get from wrestling big steers, wild mustangs, and wilder, rougher men.

The wool shirt I wore had been red at one time, but had faded, and my vest was made from the hide of a black and white cow. Nothing I wore or owned was new, and my outfit was beat-up, rained-on, and sand-weathered, and that included me too. Along with it I had a stubble of beard on a face deep-browned by the sun, and green eyes that showed up lighter than they were, against my dark skin.

I had me a fine-working Winchester and a pair of bone-handled six-shooters, only one of which was carried in sight. In my belt there was a bowie knife, and down the back of my neck a throwing knife, both of them Tinker-made.

This outfit I'd come upon was no rawhide bunch. The wagon showed travel signs, but it had been new not long ago, and both of these folks were dressed mighty well.

I hooked a knee around the pommel of the saddle, rested the muzzle of the Winchester in their general direction across my knee, and started to build myself a smoke.

"You all going somewhere," I said, "or do you like it here?"

"I'm sorry," the man said, "I am afraid we made the wrong impression."

"And you've been keeping the wrong comp'ny. Like the man who drove off your stock."

"What do you know about that?"

"Well, it's fair to surmise you didn't haul that wagon here by yourselves, and now you've got no stock."

"Indians might have taken them."

"It ain't likely. They'd have had your scalps too. No, it was somebody in your own outfit, somebody who figured to leave you high and dry out here on the cap rock; so you reckoned to kill me and ride out of here on my horse."

"We thought you were an Indian," the girl said.

Now, anybody could see a mile off that I was no Injun; but it wasn't just the lie that bothered me, it was the casual way they had set themselves out to kill a stranger. They didn't plan to ask me to ride for help, they just simply planned murder. That man had been bedded down for an ambush. Had I gone riding right up to the wagon at that girl's wave, I'd be dead by now and they would be riding out of here on my horse.

Wary as I was, I was also curious. What had brought them to this place? Who were they? Where had they come from? Where were they going? And why had their man left them and taken all their stock?

That last question provided its own answer. Either he was afraid of them, or he wanted what was in that wagon. If the last was true, the easiest way to get it was simply to drive off their stock and stay out of the way until they died or were killed. The fact that they were in this place at all gave some weight to this last theory, for they were right in the middle of nowhere, on the road to nowhere. Nobody in his right mind would have come this way with a wagon.

"Get down and join us," the man said. "We were just about to have coffee."

"Don't mind if I do," I said, swinging down, the horse between me and them. "This is mighty dry country."

My comment brought no reaction from them, which improved my hunch that they had no idea of the fix they were in. For there was no water anywhere around. They had two barrels slung to the side of the wagon, but I figured they weren't anywheres near full, and the nearest water—if there was any there—was a good forty miles away.

"You folks got yourselves in a peck of trouble," I commented. "You'll be lucky to get out of here alive."

They both looked at me, just looked, as if trying to understand me. "What do you mean by that?" the girl asked.

"Nearest water I know of is forty miles from here . . . if the creek ain't dry, which it sometimes is. If it's dry, you got twenty miles further to go. Even if you could haul the wagon—which you can't—it would mean days from here. You're way off the trail."

"It's a short cut."

"Whoever told you that had no love for you. The only place this will short-cut you to is the dry side of hell."

They both were looking hard at me.

"Your best chance is to try walking out," I said. "At best you got a fifty-fifty chance."

"But there's your horse." He gave me a cool look. "My sister and I could share it."

Now, I've come up against some mean folks in my time, but nobody quite as cool about it as these. They were in trouble, but they either had no realization of how much trouble, or they were almighty sure of themselves.

"You ain't got my horse, *amigo*," I said, "and you ain't about to get him. And if you had him, you'd not know which way to go.

If you knew where to go, you wouldn't have come here in the first place."

They exchanged a glance. They did not believe me, and they still wanted that horse of mine.

"You've got a chance," I added, "if I ride out of here and send somebody back with a team to haul the wagon out. That's if I can find somebody who's willing to come out here.

"This here is Comanche country," I went on. "Kiowas to the north, and Apaches west and south. Nobody wants to come into this country at all."

All of a sudden I had a feeling. They were not worried, because they were waiting for something, or somebody. Something they *knew* would happen. Nothing I had said had impressed them in the least. They were simply waiting.

The afternoon was almost gone, and it lacked only a few hours until darkness. Was there somebody else out there? Somebody I had not seen or heard?

Suddenly the itchy feet of fear were crawling right up my back. Somebody was out there, somewhere, watching me.

"The closest place for you is Borregos Plaza," I said, "or maybe Fort Bascom, over west of here." All the time I was trying to figure which way trouble would come from.

They were eastern folk, but I wouldn't think of them as tenderfeet. There was much they didn't know of the West, if they knew anything at all about it, but they had a quality about them ... they were ice-hard and without mercy. I had me a hunch that when in doubt they would kill, without rhyme or reason.

The company I'd known since leaving the mountains, and much of it before that, had been hard company. Feuding and fighting men, hard-working and hard-drinking men often enough, but they had fought from anger or for pay; and when they killed it was from anger or for pay, or perhaps, by blunder, but not as these two would kill.

The girl had poured a cup of coffee for me. I'd been making believe to loosen the cinch on the saddle, but had not done so. I had an idea that when I left out of there it would be of a sudden with no time to tighten a cinch.

Turning my horse, I walked toward her, keeping the horse between me and where I suspected their man to be, if man there was. Close to the fire I stopped and squatted on my heels, and glanced quickly over to where I thought he was at, and just as my eyes shifted I saw that girl shove something back in the pocket of her skirt.

Now, nothing in my life led me to be what you'd call a trusting man. Back in the Tennessee hills we did a sight of swapping, and a boy soon learned that when it came to swapping he couldn't trust even his own kin. It was a game, sort of, and we all swapped back and forth and the best stories told around the cracker barrel in the store at the crossroads or around a cabin fire were about swaps and swapping, and about who got taken. This just naturally made you grow up sort of skeptical.

So when that dewy-eyed girl handed me that coffee I took it, longing for a swallow, but just a mite afraid it might be my last. So I held it, wondering how a man could keep from drinking it without arousing suspicions.

Back on Clinch Mountain there was an old-timer who could set and talk by the hour and not say a word a body could recall; he would just ramble on spreading words around like a man forking hay on a stack. Right then I decided to talk.

"'Bout the time I sighted you folks I was gettin' fed to the teeth with my own company, and there's just so much you can say to a horse. You never talked to a horse? Ma'am, you just ain't ridden far in lonesome country. Why, I'd reach out to say the horses of this man's territory know more about what's going on than anybody else. Everybody out here talks to his horse. I've seen the time I hadn't nobody else to talk to, weeks on end.

"You take this here country now. A man can ride for days and not see even a hump in the ground, let alone a man or a horse. Maybe you'd sight some antelope, or a herd of buffalo, although they are coming up scarce about now. A body can just ride on and on across the country, watching far-off rain squalls or maybe buzzards. Not much else to see.

"And traveling in this area ain't just what you're expecting. Now you folks, for instance. You head west from here, and what do you find? A canyon maybe three, four hundred feet deep. It's cap-rock country, so usually where the land breaks off there's a drop of four to fourteen feet of sheer rock, then a steep slope off to the bottom, and you may go miles before you can find a spot to go down into the canyon, or a place to climb out.

"You never see those canyons until you're right on top of them. Comanches used to hole up in them and wait for the Comancheros coming out from Santa Fe to trade with 'em. I come upon an Indian camp one time when there must have been seven or eight thousand head of horses there—fine stock, some of them."

Both of them were watching me. I was holding the cup in my hand, gesturing with it once in a while, just running off at the mouth like that old coot back in the hills.

"You take Indians now, they're all around you before you know they're in the country. And women folks—if they know you got a woman along, they'll hunt you for miles.

"You people here, you're ripe for the picking. Any Comanche youngster could shoot you both before you even knew he were near. I'd say without help you ain't got a chance of getting out of here.

"You figure on my horse? Why, he couldn't carry the both of you even half the distance you got to go. And your wagon would have to be left where it is. Take a six-ox team to move that out of here, heavy like it is."

"What makes you think our wagon is heavy?"

Me, I grinned at him, and shoved my hat back a mite with the lip of the cup. "Why, your tracks. The deep bite they take into the prairie tells a body that. Moreover, I'd lay a bet the Indians know where you are, and are closing in about now."

"Don't be silly," the girl said. "If they knew where we were and wanted to attack they would have done it long since."

I chuckled. "That's your thinkin', but it ain't Injun thinkin'. You take those Indians now, to speak proper of them—they know you ain't going no place. They know where that canyon is up ahead, and they know what you'll have to do when you get there. Meanwhile you're getting closer and closer to where they want you. They probably have a camp some place up ahead, and when you get close enough so they won't have to pack all they take from you for any distance, why, they'll move in."

Of a sudden I glanced at my coffee. "Well, what d' you know? I been settin' here talkin' until my coffee's gone cold."

And as I said it I splashed the coffee on the ground, set down the cup, and picked up the coffeepot with my left hand. My right still held my Winchester. I filled the cup about a third full, sloshed it about and dumped it again. "Warms the cup," I said. "I do shy from coffee in a cold cup." Then I refilled it and sat back on my heels. "Now, where was I?"

Well, their faces were a study. They didn't know whether I was smart to them, or just dumb. He was exasperated, but she was so mad she turned a little pale. I gulped down some of the hot coffee and it tasted good—kind of a chicory taste to it, like some of that New Orleans make.

Setting there a-drinking my coffee, seeming to pay them no mind, nor nothing else, I wasn't much worried. I could see over east toward where that canyon was from the tail of my eye, one of the quickest ways to detect movement, and I was keeping my horse within my range of vision. Shadows were growing on the lee side of that wagon, when of a sudden my mustang's ears pricked and I put my cup down.

That mustang, like all wild stock, was quick to see anything that moved. Most horses are quick enough to see and hear, but there's nothing like a wild one for letting you know when trouble's about. His ears warned me that whoever was out there had begun to move.

Any sudden move of mine to get away would bring on the fight I wanted to avoid. I didn't cater to these folks' way of figuring things, and I didn't aim to let them take my scalp.

There was little cover out on those grasslands, and even the grass was skimpy, so if I tried to ride for it I would have two or maybe three of them shooting at me. Unless I waited until dark... though every minute I waited increased my own risk, for darkness gave them freedom of movement.

So I just shifted my Winchester forward in my hands and looked at that young man standing over there beside his sister, and I said, "If you two figure to get where you're going all in one piece, you better tell your friend out there to stand up and come in with his hands up."

That set them back a notch. They just looked at me, and I eased back the hammer on the Winchester.

He turned a shade paler and said, "I don't know what you mean."

"You just speak up and tell him. You got a full thirty seconds to do it in, or I'll spread you wide open for the buzzards and the ants."

He didn't want to believe it, and when he decided he'd better he still didn't want to.

"It'll be you first," I said, "and then the girl and the other one. You got ten seconds now, and I'm takin' up slack."

My finger tightened on the trigger.

TWO

"Andrew," the girl spoke out loud and clear, "come in with your hands up."

"Sylvie," her brother protested, "he wouldn't shoot. He wouldn't dare."

"He'll shoot, all right!" Sylvie said. "He would kill you very quickly, Ralph, and I believe he would kill me too."

There was a stir out in the darkness, and then a fat, stupid-looking boy came in toward us. He might have been only seventeen, but the rifle he carried was grown up.

"Put it down," I said to him, but I was prepared for him to try a shot. He looked at me, then shifted his eyes toward Sylvie... toward her, not toward her brother.

"Do what he says, Andrew."

Reluctantly, he put down the rifle, then sat down abruptly and crossed his legs.

"Like I said, I don't want any trouble, but I've grown up with it. My advice to you folks is to go slow. You'll find things are different out here, and there's a lot of folks who will shoot first and ask questions later, if they have any to ask.

"Now, if you'll lay off trying to shoot me, I'll see if I can get you out of here."

"Why should you?" Ralph asked.

On that one I hedged. After all, why not ride out and leave them to get what they deserved? "You've got guns," I said. "I wouldn't want them in the hands of the Indians."

They didn't believe me. I doubt if they could believe any reason that was not entirely selfish.

"No matter which way you go, you ain't likely to find anybody inside of a hundred miles. I hear Jim Cator has a buffalo camp on the North Palo Duro, and the settlements west are nearer to two hundred miles than one."

14

They sat watching me, taking in every word.

"Whoever brought you in here trapped you for fair...but there's a chance I might catch up to him and bring the horses back."

"If you could bring those horses back," Ralph said, "and kill the thief who stole them, I would give you fifty dollars."

"There's some who would do it for that," I commented, "but I am not one. However, it would be easier to get your horses back than to ride out and send somebody in for you." I stood up suddenly. "I'll ride after him."

They all stood up at that, their eyes on me, ready to take any advantage. "Why not stay and try in the morning?" Sylvie suggested. "You can't track horses at night."

Stepping up, I took the bridle and turned my horse to watch them across the saddle, and then I mounted quickly, my rifle ready, covering them casually. "I don't need to track them," I replied. "He'll take them to water. I'll follow."

Swinging the horse, I rode a widening half-circle around the camp, keeping them under my gun until I was well into the darkness, then quickly I switched direction and walked my horse until I had put a good distance behind me. When I was a mile off I drew up and took off my hat and wiped the sweat-band. For a while there they had me treed.

Then I set off through the night, taking my course from the stars. I had a fair idea where those horses would be, and if they were there, I'd look the situation over before making a move. I had no use for that lot back there, but I couldn't leave a woman to die out on the plains, nor did I want those guns in the hands of Indians, who had enough guns as it was.

The night was cool, and despite the fact my horse was tired, I kept him moving, and he was game enough. I don't think he'd liked that bunch any more than I had.

At times I got down and walked to save the horse. The dun had come far that day, for I had pushed him hard since early morning, but I had a hunch. There was a place in the cap rock that I knew of... I'd been told of it by a Comanchero who had watered there at times when driving from Santa Fe over to a rendezvous with the Comanches.

It was a mere gap in the rock forty or fifty yards wide, and scarcely longer, but there was water in the bottom, a little grass, and a cottonwood tree or two. There was a chance that the man I followed knew of it too, although few did. If he could water there, he could drive the stock north, and after another fifteen miles or so would come upon a series of small hollows fringed with cottonwoods and willows where there were fresh water lakes, or sloughs. From that time on he could move toward Tule Creek, with water to be found at intervals all along the way.

The last bright stars were hanging low in the sky when I came up to the water hole. There was the low, questioning nicker from a horse, and a sudden movement, then silence.

My move was just as quick. Leaving the dun standing, reins trailing, I ducked off to the left where a cottonwood made a shadow on the land, and I crouched there, waiting.

Slowly, the moments passed. The dun, weary of waiting when water was so close, walked a few steps toward the hollow, holding his head off to one side to keep from stepping on the reins. This was what I had expected would happen, and what I wanted to happen. Whoever was waiting would be likely to think it was a stray horse. Or so I hoped.

The dun was all mustang, however, and not one to go right down into the hollow. He pricked his ears and whinnied a bit, and from the hollow there was an answering whinny. After a moment the dun walked on, then stopped again. Only this time he stopped because he was close to somebody.

Not moving a muscle, I waited. And then I heard a low, coaxing voice. He was trying to call my horse close enough to lay hand to the reins. The dun, knowing I was out and about, was not likely to let a strange hand reach him. Had he been a stray, lost and wandering, he might have let himself be caught...at least as long as he had that saddle on him.

Suddenly the dun shied away...evidently the man had tried to reach for him, which meant he was growing impatient.

The dun backed off a step and stood there, and I just waited. Five, maybe ten minutes went by, and then the man stepped from the darkness and reached for the reins. The horse backed off a couple of steps, and I could have kissed him, for the man went after him.

"Hold it!" I spoke loud enough for him to hear, but not too loud, and as I spoke I cocked my rifle.

He made a move as if to dive for shelter, but I spoke again, quickly. "Don't try! You ain't got a chance."

"Who are you?"

"A driftin' man. That there's my horse."

"Thought he was strayed." I had gotten to my feet and started toward him as he spoke. "Didn't see anybody around."

"Hadn't planned on it. Don't get nervous now... I'm holding a light trigger."

He had turned and was facing me, a stocky, barrel-chested man with his face in shadow. Suddenly he spoke. "Hell, you're Nolan Sackett!"

"Unbuckle your belt."

"Now, see here—"

I was getting impatient. "Mister, if you figure on eatin' breakfast, you'd better drop that gun belt."

He reached for the buckle, protesting. "Now look, Sackett. I'm Steve Hooker. We met one time over in the Nation, an' you got no call to stand me up."

"Maybe, maybe not."

When he'd unbuckled his gun belt and dropped it, I had him back off while I moved in and took up the belt and slung it over my shoulder.

Gathering the dun's reins, I followed my prisoner back down into the hollow. The horses were there, a fine team of six head, and two saddle horses. Down among the willows he had a fire going that had not been visible from the cap rock. I could smell coffee, and realized I'd not had a mouthful of food all day.

Once we got into the firelight I had him face around, and I knew him all right. He had been a teamster for a freight outfit, fired for selling stock feed that belonged to the company. He had killed a tame Indian over at Fort Griffin one time. Nobody did anything about it, but nobody had any use for him after that.

I turned him around and lashed his hands together behind his back, then tied his ankles and his knees. After setting him where I could keep an eye on him, I stripped the rig from my dun and let him roll, then rubbed him down carefully with a few handfuls of dried grass. Then I put him on a picket line where he could graze, and let him go to water as he wished.

Getting a slab of bacon from my pack, I shaved slices into a pan and broke out a half a loaf of bakery bread, brought from town.

Whilst I was frying it, I poured myself a cup of coffee and made idle talk about the Indian Territory.

"Where'd you get the team?" I asked suddenly.

"They're mine. Drivin' 'em west to sell in New Mexico."

I just looked at him, disgusted. "That's a mighty pretty story to tell a pilgrim," I said, "but nobody in his right mind comes alone into this country, especially with horses." And then I added, "I rode in from the south."

He made no comment about that, although he was doing some thinking, wondering whether I'd seen the wagon or not. "How did you find me?" he said, after a bit.

"You left tracks, and I followed them." And then I added, "You also left a woman back there, where she could be taken by Indians."

"That ain't no woman! She's a blasted devil! She's a witch right out of hell."

"Looked young an' pretty to me. Didn't seem any place to leave a couple of tenderfeet." I paused, turned the bacon over with a fork, and then added, "You could get lynched for that."

"They'd of killed me. They were fixing to. I heard 'em talk of it."

"Where did you pick them up?"

He hesitated. "I seen 'em first in Fort Worth. They were dressed elegant and seemed to have money. I sort of listened around and heard him making inquiries about the country west of Griffin."

"So?"

He peered at me. "Now look, Sackett. You ain't no fool. Why would a couple of well-dressed tenderfeet like them be interested in this country? This is buffalo country, Indian country. It's also cattle country, or so some think; but there's no fancy hotels and nothing to attract folks of that kind."

"What's your idea?"

"Gold, that's what. Gold, and lots of it. You think they'd come looking for range land, them folks? Not on your bottom dollar. Whatever they're huntin' is something they can carry away, and I think the answer to it is in that wagon."

"What's in it?"

"Now that's an odd thing. They never did let me see, and I tried. Maybe that's why they figured to kill me."

"Where were they headed?"

Steve Hooker was silent, probably deciding how much he should tell and how much he should hold back. Meanwhile, I started eating the bacon and fried bread right out of the frying pan. I was hungry enough to eat pan and all, but had to settle for about a dozen slices of thick bacon and the half-loaf of bread fried in bacon grease. And I drank most of Hooker's coffee.

"You better tell me," I went on, refilling my cup for the last time, "I ain't made up my mind whether to take you back to them, or let you waste away right here. You talk fast an' right and maybe you'll get a chance."

"What kind of talk is that? There's a good thing in this . . . for both of us."

Well, now. I felt a sight better. I set back against the bank and watched my horse pulling at the green grass, feeling almighty pleased with the world. Still, I had this man tied up and I was of no mind to trust him untied, especially as I was sleepy.

"What questions did they ask you?"

"Oh, they knew something, all right. I think they had read something or heard something, but they had special knowledge too. I mean they knew where they wanted to go."

He gave it to me, a little at a time. He had followed them when they went from Fort Worth to Fort Griffin by stage. Actually, he had ridden the stage with them, keeping his mouth shut and listening to the questions they asked. The girl had been very good at getting a couple of western men to talking; above all, she seemed interested in place names . . . thought they were so colorful, she said.

"Like what?" I asked.

"Cross Timbers . . . the Llano Estacado . . . Boggy Depot . . . the Rabbit Ears."

Hooker hitched himself around a little, but I paid him no mind. He was hinting that I should loosen him up a little, which I wasn't about to do. "She got them to talk about those places."

"Ask any questions?"

"Full of 'em. She asked questions half the night. Her brother finally went to sleep, but not her. She kept prying away at what those men knew, but what she kept coming back to was the Rabbit Ears."

I went to the edge of the willows and broke up some sticks and twisted some dead limbs off a fallen cottonwood. When I came back I started feeding the fire again and made another pot of coffee. I knew a thing or two about the Rabbit Ears country, and I'd heard some stories. More than likely, bunkhouse talk being what it was, Steve Hooker had heard the same tales. And like he said, there was no good reason for anybody like those folks to want to go into such country.

"You sure took them far off the route," I commented dryly, "where they'd meet nobody who could tell them different."

"When we got to Griffin," Hooker said, "I approached her, told her as how I'd heard she wanted a wagon man, and I was a man who knew the country to the west. Upshot of it was, she bought the horses and wagon, outfitted us complete."

He looked around at me. "She had me spooked, that girl did. And he was almost as bad. I don't know what it was, nothing they did or said, but she kept a-watching me and it kind of got me.

"Then one night I heard them talking. They thought I'd taken the stock off to water, and so I had, but I snuck back to listen. First thing I heard her say was 'Of course. Why waste our money on him? When we get to the Rabbit Ears we'll know our way back, so we'll kill him.' Thing that got me was she was so matter of fact about it, like she'd ask the time of day.

"Next morning I began to pull off south. I figured to get them lost so they'd never find their way back by themselves, and would need me. Then I got to thinkin'."

"I know," I said, "you got to thinking about that outfit. You got to figuring what it would bring you at Cherry Creek, or even Santa Fe. Six head of fine horses, a brand new wagon, and whatever they had inside."

"Well, what of it? They were fixin' to kill me."

"How'd you manage? Weren't they suspicious?"

"You're darn tootin' they were! They watched me all the time. On'y I told them we would make camp half a mile from water . . . too many mosquitoes."

"Then you came on to this place?"

"Sure. Them tenderfeet would never find it. I on'y had to wait. Just set still an' wait."

"What about Rabbit Ears?"

"Who knows anything? She worried around that subject, but nobody had anything to offer except me, and I kept my mouth shut, on'y just saying enough to make 'em ready to talk to me when the time came."

"What did you say?"

"That Rabbit Ears was named for an old Injun chief. That was every bit I said."

There was no logical reason for anybody to come out from the East just to visit Rabbit Ears Mountain. As mountains went, it was nothing very much. Not too far west there were real mountains covered with timber, and much of the year with snow. Rabbit Ears Mountain lay just off the Santa Fe Trail, and was no more striking than many another hill or mountain. Of course, her questions might have masked some other interest in the country nearby.

After a bit Hooker interrupted my thoughts. "What do you figure to do?"

"I'm taking their horses back. After that, it's up to them."

"What about me?"

"You get out of here the best way you can. You're no pilgrim. You got yourself into this."

"You'd set me afoot out here?"

"No." I grinned at him. "You can go back to work for them, if you're of a mind to. When a man starts out on something like you started he takes his own chances."

The firelight danced weirdly against the dark, fragile arms of the willows. Walking over to my saddle, I got my blanket and poncho and brought it back to a place near the fire, but in the shadows. I added fuel to the fire, pulled off my boots, and prepared to settle down for the night. From my pack I took a pair of moccasins and pulled them on . . . in the night I might have to make a quick move, with no chance to get my boots on.

Then I went over and released Hooker and let him move around a little before I tied him for the night. He was a wily one, and I stood back away from him and kept my rifle in hand.

After he was tied up again and covered with his blanket, I went back and rolled up to sleep. When I fell asleep I was still giving thought to the Rabbit Ears, and what those folks might want out there. Oddly enough, I'd never even heard the name those folks used . . . and it might make a difference.

Although in the West we set no store on names.

THREE

At daybreak I walked Hooker out on the cap rock with a canteen, a pack of grub, and his guns. His gun belts I took with me and rode off maybe three hundred yards, where I dropped them for him to pick up. Then I gathered the horses and started back.

Now, I was in no way anxious to be riding back to that outfit. In a way I had no blame for Hooker, although I'd leave no woman out there a prey to Indians, nor did I aim to give them a chance at me.

In my time I'd known a few killers, but I'd never known anybody quite as anxious to kill as these folks. Even when it was of no particular use to them. Whatever it was they were after, they didn't want anybody interfering with them, or even knowing what they were about.

Well, I wasn't going to play nurse to them. I liked my sleep too well. They would have the team, and if they got out of there they would do it under their own power and by their own skill.

The girl came out to meet me. She was bait, I had no doubt, and believe me, that Sylvie was tasty bait for any man's trap, and she knew it. She walked out when she saw me coming, skirting the clumps of prickly pear or the prairie-dog holes. And then she stopped until I rode up to her.

Only my rifle was laid across my saddle bows, just sort of casual-like, but the muzzle kind of followed her when she moved. But she brought her hands into the open where I could see them, and kept them there.

"Here's your horses," I told her, "and the rest is up to you. You take my advice and you'll turn back to Fort Griffin. You don't fit into this country."

She smiled at me. "Why, Mr. Sackett! I thought you liked me?"

"You're a mighty pretty girl, Sylvie, and just about as safe as a nest of rattlers. But you take it from me and cut out of this country. Go east, where you belong."

She came closer, looking up at me with those big, dark eyes. "Come with us. Please do. We need you, Mr. Sackett, we're all alone out here, and neither of the boys has ever driven a team." She reached up and touched my hand with her fingers. "Mr. Sackett, come with us. Believe me, you'd never be sorry... and I'd be very grateful."

Well, now. She wasn't promising me anything, but in a way she was promising me everything, and she was quite a woman, that one. Only I wasn't having any.

"Sorry," I said. "Maybe if you were alone; but I'd trust none of you. You've got the horses. Hitch up and pull out right away, and follow my tracks. You'll come to water, and you'd better fill your barrels. They should help you over the dry stretch, and after that there's water most of the way north. Only you're going to run into the Palo Duro Canyon... maybe a thousand feet deep in places."

"Are there no ranchers? No towns?"

"Lady, this here is Indian country. You won't even find any buffalo hunters until you get farther north. There's said to be some folks at Borregos Plaza on the south bank of the Canadian. They're good folks, Mexicans from Mora or Taos, and they run sheep. If you act right, they'll sell you a little food and tell you how to get on to the north.

"I say they're good people, and they are, but there's one hombre from Santa Fe named Sostenes l'Archeveque... he'd kill you as soon as look at you. He idles around there from time to time... leave him alone."

All the time I'd been talking to her I'd been holding her right hand. A time or two she gave it a tug to get free, but I decided it was safer that way and, holding her right hand, I kept my eyes watching the other two. Finally I dropped her hand.

"*Adios!*" I said suddenly, and wheeled and rode off.

I gave my horse about three jumps north before I turned him sharply east, then west. Glancing back, I caught the gleam of light on a rifle barrel, but by that time I was another hundred yards off and a poor risk for a shot at the distance, and moving the way I was. So I rode away, and was glad to be gone.

About that time I began to give thought to myself. Here I was, riding away from trouble, no more than eight or nine dollars in my pocket, and nothing more in sight. For a man with the name of outlaw, I was doing mighty poor at it. When it came to that, I never did see any rich outlaws. All I ever saw were living on the dodge, out on the plains, in the mountains, or in outlaw hide-outs, ragged, dirty, and miserable.

Buffalo hunting was about over. In no time at all the hunters would have wiped out the buffalo in this country, and would pull out. What I should do was to get myself a few head of cattle and start myself a ranch right here in the Panhandle of Texas. It would be no time at all until cattle were streaming into this country. The buffalo hunters would be telling of the good grass and the water holes, and no cattleman would ask for more.

I had the name of being a rough man, and that came of the troubles I'd seen, and the fact that I'd come out of them winning instead of losing. This was a time of bitter war and struggle, for the Indian gave up his hunting grounds reluctantly, and even those of us in sympathy with him were compelled to fight, because they could not always distinguish between friends and enemies. Of course, it wasn't only the white man fighting the Indian, for the Indians were constantly at war with each other.

Now I drifted north, holding to the high ridges, where I rode just below the crest, out of sight yet high enough to ride easy and keep a wide view of the country. When I saw dust, I drew up and got down and waited until it had gone out of sight, for though it might be white men raising the dust, I'd no reason to think they would be friendly.

All the time, my mind was being busy trying to remember all I'd heard of the Rabbit Ears, and the one thing I kept coming back to was a story I'd heard trail-side down on the Neuces seven or eight years back.

The story was already old, and the man who told it to me was a Mexican from across the Rio Grande. He had hailed my camp from out of the night, and I told him to come in. That was brush country, and rougher than a cob; every other man an outlaw or a renegade hiding out from the Davis police.

John Wesley Hardin was on the dodge then, and Bill Longley, just to name two. Up in northeast Texas Cullen Baker was dead, or at least they said they had killed him, and he never showed up around after that. All these men were refugees from the Davis police.

I had stepped back in the shadows to let that Mex come in, and he came politely, with his hands up. He was an oldish man, but dapper and mighty elegant still. His boots were dusty, and although he had tried to brush himself off there was trail-dust on him.

"Señor?"

Well, I stepped out of the brush. By and large I'd found Mexicans the salt of the earth, and many a time when on the dodge the only thing that kept me alive was a bait of frijoles and tortillas at some Mexican sheep camp.

"Come in and set," I said. "There's coffee ready and beans in the pot."

So we ate, and then he rolled him a smoke and we yarned the night away. He was afoot... he didn't say how or why, and in those days a body didn't ask questions. It happened I had an extra horse, a paint pony, pretty as a picture. A few days before that pony had been ridden by a mighty handsome young Comanche with bad judgment. He was riding loose, hunting for some action, and when he saw me he exercised that bad judgment... he decided I was easy pickings and fell in on my trail. Only I was keeping an eye on my back trail and when I saw I was followed I circled around and hunched down close to the trail to see who it was.

When I saw it was a Comanche with two fresh scalps, I stepped out and spoke to him. He turned as if he was shot and started to lift his rifle, which was his second case of bad judgment, for I only figured to set him afoot so he couldn't follow me any longer.

He put hand to that rifle and I shot him through the brisket, emptying the paint pony's saddle like there'd never been anything there. The Comanche was game; he came up fighting, so I let him have another one, caught up the pony, and left out of the country.

"You need a horse," I said to the Mexican; "you take that one. The Comanche who owned him won't be hunting him."

"Gracias, señor." He spoke simply, yet with feeling, and he had a right. In that country at that time the only folks he was apt to meet would more than likely finish him off for his guns or whatever else he might have.

We drank more coffee and talked, and then at the last he said, "*Amigo*, I have no money. I cannot pay for the horse."

"He is yours, think nothing of it."

"My grandfather," he said, "used to drive mules on the Santa Fe Trail."

Well, now. That was an interesting bit of information if I'd been interested in his grandfather, which I wasn't, or in the Santa Fe Trail, which I'd seen my ownself.

"It was there he nearly lost his life. He was *jefe* of a pack train for Nathan Hume."

It all came back to me now, and I recalled as if it had been last night, us sitting by the fire and him telling me about that pack train. They had come from Santa Fe, and were crossing the plains, bound for Independence, Missouri, or some such place, and they had been making good time until they were hit by a war party of Kiowas.

They were strung out too far, and they didn't have much chance. A few of them gathering around Nathan Hume himself, among them my Mexican friend's grandfather, bunched up and made a retreating fight of it back to the Rabbit Ears Mountain, where they dug in for a stand.

They were wiped out...all but that Mexican, who found a hole and crawled into it. The Kiowas scalped and mutilated the bodies after robbing them of everything worth having, and then rode off a-running. After a bit that Mex came out and hoofed it back to Santa Fe.

When he got back he was warned to lie low, that the governor had sent a detachment of soldiers after Hume, and that if he were found he would be arrested. Nathan Hume had been smuggling gold secretly mined in the San Juans. So this Mexican smuggled himself out of town on a borrowed mule and then joined a train headed for Mexico City. He had friends there, and he planned to get some help and return, for he was sure he knew where the gold was...and was sure the Indians had not found it.

The trouble was, shortly after arriving in Mexico he was thrown from a horse. His back was broken and he never walked again.

He knew where three hundred pounds of gold was hidden, and he couldn't do a thing about it.

This was the story that was told to me by the Mex to whom I'd given a horse.

"Did you ever give thought to hunting that gold?" I'd asked him.

"Of course, señor, but"—he shrugged—"I had a difficulty in Taos...a matter of a señorita...and I was followed to Las Vegas. I killed a man, señor, a man with many brothers and cousins and uncles."

He put his cigarette in the fire and smiled. "I like life, señor, and I am a man who is content with a little now and another time. If I went north I *might* find the gold. I might also find a grave, and the odds for the latter are best. If you want the gold it is yours, señor."

"Any idea where it is?"

"There's a box canyon back of Rabbit Ears. It was there they made their stand...the bones of the mules might be there still.

"There was a pool of water there, covered with a green moss or scum, and beyond the pool a hole under a boulder. The gold was hidden in the hole, rocks tumbled over it, and with a broken gun Nathan Hume chipped a cross on the boulder. You should find it."

The next morning we parted, and once in the saddle he held out his hand to me and we shook hands. "Be careful, señor, and ask no questions. The Mexicans who mined the gold had sons and grandsons, and they know that Nathan Hume's mule train did not get to Missouri...they might even have spoken to the Indians."

It was not the first trail-side story I'd heard of buried gold or lost mines. Such stories were told and retold all up and down the country, although this was the first time I'd heard this one. But I kept it in mind, and planned to take a look for myself sometime. Only things kept happening.

In Serbin, a town of Wendish folk in Texas where I'd had friends, I killed a carpetbagger and was thrown in jail for it. But my Wendish friends found a way to help me escape and left my horse where I could find it. I joined up with a trail herd headed for the Kansas towns, but I was a man wanted by the law.

In Abilene, which was new, raw, and wild, I found my name was known. There'd been a cousin of mine there named Tyrel and he'd killed a man in the streets, somebody said; but then I got the straight of it. He had faced down Reed Carney, walked up to him, and made him drop his gun belt into the street.

Tyrel and Orrin Sackett—I'd heard tell of them, although they came from the Cumberland Gap country; but it gave me a rarely good feeling to know the Sackett blood ran true.

That was long ago, and now I was here, riding north in the Panhandle of Texas, riding over the Staked Plains and heading north toward Borregos Plaza, Adobe Walls, and the buffalo camps. I was riding a line-back dun across the plains where a man could stand in his stirrups and look straight away for three days, it was that level.

So I shoved my rifle down in the boot, I canted my hat back on my head, and I looked off across the country and opened my mouth in song. At least, I felt it was song, and tried to make it that way, although the dun wasn't sure. The sky was blue and the plains were wide, and there was land around to stretch in. Maybe I'd only a few dollars in my jeans and a hanging party left behind, but the wind smelled good and the sun was warm, and it was a great time to be alive.

The country around me began to break up again into softly rolling hills, with a few ridges and some hollows where there were trees.

"Oh, I left my girl in San Antone,
Away down near the border,
I—"

A tuft of feathers showed over the crest of a low hill, and a dozen yards away an Indian appeared, and then another and another. A broken line of Kiowas stretched out for two hundred yards. They were riding slowly toward me, their lances pointed skyward. I glanced around quickly, and across the valley there were half a dozen more riding toward me, walking their horses.

At least a dozen of them had rifles, and they seemed in no hurry. Down the valley the way lay open, but several of the Indians were further along than I was, and they had only to cut over and head me off. There were at least thirty Indians in the whole party, and they had me boxed.

Sweat broke out on my forehead, but my mouth was dry. I had seen what Kiowas could do to a prisoner, for I had come upon what was left when they had finished, and it was no sight for a man with a weak stomach.

If I tried to make a run for it I would be dead within a minute.

Turning my horse at right angles, I rode straight for them, still singing.

FOUR

My rifle was in the boot, and to reach for it would mean death. My pistol, in its holster, was held down by the thong hooked over the hammer, a necessity when riding rough country.

So I rode straight for them, pointing the dun to ride right between two of them who rode some thirty yards apart, and singing as I rode.

Nobody ever figured a way to account for the thinking of an Indian. They were curious as any wild animal, and at times as temperamental, but the thing they admired most was courage, because you needed courage to be a good Indian. I knew I wouldn't get anywhere now trying to run; and when it comes to that, I am not a man who cares to run, unless it's *toward* something.

That dun pricked up his ears. He knew we were in trouble, and he didn't like the smell of Indians; I could feel every muscle in him poised with eagerness to take out and run.

These braves weren't hunting me. They were a war party all right, and they were out for bigger game. But if they were fixing for trouble with me they were going to get it. As I walked my horse toward them I made up my mind what to do. The big Indian on the right was my meat. If they made a hostile move I'd jump my horse into him, and grab for my pistol. I went through the motions in my mind, and all the while I was singing about that girl I left in San Antone.

Behind me I could hear the riders closing in, and in front of me they had slowed their horses a little, but I kept right on riding. My right hand was on my thigh, where it had been all along, only inches from the butt of my gun. I knew that if I got my gun out before they killed me I wouldn't go alone. If there was one thing I could do well in this world it was shoot a pistol.

Back in the Clinch Mountains in the fifties and sixties a boy

30

just naturally cut his teeth on guns, and before I was twelve years old I'd been out in the woods feeding the family with a rifle, and with little time for anything else.

My eyes held straight ahead, yet I was watching the Indian on either side of me. There were a-plenty of others there, but it was those two who would bring on the trouble and they were coming closer and closer. My spur was just caressing that bronc's flank, ready to nudge him into action.

Those Indians came right on and I rode right toward them. Of a sudden the one on my left brought his lance down slowly, pointing it at me, but I never flinched. Had I showed one sign of the scare that was in me, he'd have run me through, or tried it.

He put the point of that lance right against my chest, and I looked over it and right into his eyes. I put my left hand up, still holding the reins, and pushed the point aside, just nice and easy, and then I walked my horse right on past.

Believe me, the skin was crawling up my back and the hair on the back of my neck was prickling, but I didn't dare take a look back. Suddenly there was a rustle of hoofs in the grass, but a sharp command stopped them. One of those Indians, probably an old chief, had saved my bacon. I kept right on, walking my horse, the sweat dripping off my face as if I'd dipped my head under a pump.

I went right on until I had the low ridge behind me, and then I touched the dun with the spur and we lit out of there like the fires of hell were behind us.

Then I slowed, turned at right angles to my route and rode down into the bed of a small stream and followed it west for a couple of miles.

Riding in water is far from a full-proof way to hide a trail. My horse's tracks would remain in the bottom for maybe an hour or more with the stream running at that slow rate, and the water being clear as it was, so when I got upstream I caved dirt into the water at several points to muddy the stream so the tracks couldn't be seen, and also to give the stream more silt to fill in the tracks. It would take some time for the water to become clear again.

They'd let me go on, more than likely, because they respected me, or because they were hunting bigger game, but some of the young braves might change their minds and trail off after me, liking the looks of my horse or my guns.

Alternately walking or trotting my horse, I worked my way across country, keeping an eye out for any movement, and all the time wary of my back trail. Antelope were nearly always in sight, and from time to time I saw buffalo, scattered bunches of them, growing more frequent as I moved north. But I saw no more Indians.

Once I found wheel tracks, but they were months old. I took in after them and followed their trail, camping near water every night, occasionally laying over until noontime to give the dun a rest and a chance to graze.

The country grew rougher as I went on. The stubble on my face grew thicker, and my bones and muscles grew weary of riding. Sometimes it seemed as if there must be dust and sand all through me, and half the water I drank was gyp water. But every night I checked my guns, keeping them clean and ready for trouble.

Somewhere to the north, I knew, was the Mexican town of Romero. It was a little place, and had been there quite a spell. The folks there were friendly to the Indians, and some said had been Comancheros, who traded with the Indians, selling them guns in exchange for whatever the Indians had taken from the white men moving west. Nobody liked the Comancheros much, not even their own people. But I never put my stock in that story about the folks at Romero being Comancheros.

But Borregos Plaza was the first place I would come to, and I was drawing close to it—at least, the way distances go in that country.

At daybreak I dipped into the Palo Duro, feeling uneasy because this was the heart of the Comanche country; but I rested in a clump of willows until nigh on to sundown, letting the dun eat that rich green bottom grass, and drink the water there. When the shadows started reaching out, I saddled up and scouted a way out of the canyon I was in, and I breathed easier when I was back on the plains.

The tiny cantina at Borregos Plaza was bright with lights when I walked my horse up the trail to the settlement. Dogs barked, and here and there I glimpsed movement in a darkened doorway. Strangers were welcome at Borregos Plaza, but the Mexicans who lived there had learned to be wary of them, too. It was a wild, rough land, and the few men who rode there were often wild, rough men.

Swinging down in front of the cantina I tied the dun and, ducking my head, went through the door. There was a bar about twenty feet long, and four tables with chairs around them. A fat Mexican in a white shirt stood behind the bar, his forearms on the bar. Two leather-chapped vaqueros stood near him, drinking. At one of the tables sat two older men, one with white hair.

The room was small, immaculate, and cool, with that sense of spaciousness one gets from Mexican building. All eyes turned on me, a big, dusty, travel-stained man. I went up to the bar, and ordered a drink.

"You have come far, señor?"

"Too far . . . ran into a war party of Kiowas."

"You were fortunate. You are still alive."

"No figuring on Indians. I rode right through them. Nobody lifted a hand."

They exchanged glances. It took nerve to ride through a bunch of Kiowas, and they knew that if I'd shown any weakness I would be dead now. But nobody knew how scared I'd been, and I wasn't planning on telling them.

"You will be hungry, señor? If you will sit down my wife will bring food to you."

"*Gracias.*" I walked over to a table and dropped wearily into a chair, then I removed my hat and ran my fingers through my hair. I could have fallen asleep right there.

The señora brought a plate of beans, beef, and tortillas to the table, and a pot of coffee. It was late, and the others drifted out to go home. The Mexican came out from behind the bar and sat down and filled a cup with fresh coffee.

"I am called Pio. . . . You want a place to stay?"

"No . . . I've slept out so long I'd never be able to sleep inside. I'll go out under the trees."

"You won't have trouble. Those who live here are good people."

"Are there any other strangers around?"

"There was a man . . . he rode through here yesterday but he wasn't around long. He acted as if somebody was following him."

He looked up into my eyes but I grinned at him. "You got me wrong. I ain't after anybody. I'm just riding north, going up to

Romero, and then if things look good, maybe over to the Colorado mines."

He was skeptical, I could see that, but he was a good man, and he was willing to wait for any further information.

Me, I knew better than to start anything in these quiet little places. They were quiet because they were left alone. The men here, each man in each house, had a buffalo gun and he could shoot. Each man in this town had fought Indians, renegades, and whoever wanted a fight. If a man started trouble in one of these little western towns he was setting himself up at the end of a shooting gallery. Moreover, it was an even-money bet that Pio knew about the shooting down country. News like that travels fast.

After I'd eaten and had drunk a quart of coffee, I went outside and led my horse into the trees and beyond them to the meadow. Then, stripping off the saddle, I gave him a careful rubdown while he fed on a bait of corn I'd gotten from Pio. Western horses got mighty little corn, but that dun had it coming; and thinking of him made me think kindly of that old man back there who had given him to me.

Before this, I hadn't dared to strip the saddle from him for fear I might have to light out again, to light a shuck, as the saying was.

It was a quiet night. I could hear the rustle of the cottonwood leaves, and sometimes heard subdued sounds from the plaza. There was a coyote out on the knoll making music at the stars. Rolled up in my blankets, two of them, atop my poncho, I slept like a baby . . . a baby who'd never known a night in his life when there mightn't be trouble.

Sunup was a rare fine thing. Washing my face in the water that poured into the horse trough, I glanced over at the buckboard standing in front of the cantina. A Mexican was hitching a fresh team to the buckboard, and the rattle of the trace chains was the only sound in the little street, shaded by the huge old cottonwoods.

My fingers had to do for a comb, something I'd not owned in more than a year, but I saddled up before I went into my saddlebags for my razor, which I stropped on my belt. Then I shaved, using the still end of the horse trough for a mirror. It made me look some better, although I'd never win no prizes for looks, not with that broken nose of mine.

When I'd finished shaving, I dabbed whiskey on my jaws for

a shaving lotion and then led my dun across to the hitch rail. A man living my kind of life never would let himself get caught without a gun or a saddle horse.

I went inside, where Pio was standing over a table at which three people were sitting, but the first one I saw was the girl.

She was young...maybe seventeen. Most girls were married at her age, or soon after. She had kind of dark red hair and brown eyes.... She was beautiful...taller than most girls...and shaped like music.

The old man with her was rail-thin and waspish, with hard gray eyes and a gray mustache mixed with red. You could see at a glance that he was a man with no give to him, and a man that no man in his right mind would try to cross. The third man was a breed...I'd say half Indian, anyway. A slight-built man, he was, and past middle age.

When I sat down at a table Pio's wife came in with a plate of food, a heaping plate, for she had noticed the night before that I was a good feeder. She was one of those women who liked nothing better than to see a man sit up to table and put away the food.

A couple of times the old man glanced my way, and once the girl did. I heard Pio say something about "Romero..." but his voice trailed off.

Pretty soon he came over to my table and dropped into a chair. He motioned to his wife for a fresh pot of coffee and we started in on it, Pio being as good a hand at putting it away as I was myself.

"Those people," Pio said, "they go north."

"Yeah?"

"I fear for them. She is young, the señorita. And the men...good men, but not plainsmen."

"What are they doin' out here then? No man in his right mind brings a woman like that into this country."

Pio shrugged. "I brought mine. What must be done must be done. Perhaps there was no other place."

There were questions I could have asked, but it was none of my business. I was lighting out of here right soon, and more than likely I wouldn't be back this way again.

Only that pack train of Nathan Hume's kept sticking in my mind. If all that gold was up there in those mountains, maybe I should just look around. I wanted no part of that outfit I'd left behind, but it was likely I'd be there before them.

"It is said you are an outlaw, señor?"

I looked up at him, but I did not speak. It was said, but I didn't much like it.

"I think, myself, you are an honest man, and a caballero. I think you are one to be trusted."

"You think whatever you like."

"Those three... they need help."

My hand was reaching for the bean pot, but it stopped halfway. "No, you don't," I said. "Not me. I'm not being saddled with no pilgrims. Not crossing that country."

"It was a thought."

"You better give it another think. I'm a fast-travelin' man in Injun country. I want it so's I can run or hide, and you'd play hell hidin' a buckboard or its tracks. It's a far stretch from here to wherever they're headed, and I've got business up country."

"She is a pretty girl. The Comanches..."

"Too bad."

Pio was silent. Maybe he knew more about me than I wanted to admit to myself, but he just sat there and waited, and like a damned fool I looked over at that girl setting there with her pa, if that was what he was, and that breed.

She was so fresh and young and pretty that I had to look away fast or soon I'd be doing just what Pio wanted, and making a fool of myself. Yet a body couldn't see her setting there looking so young and lovely without thinking what would happen to her if the Comanches got her.

Now, back east where the Indians are tame and mighty few, a lot of folks have started talking about the poor red man, but believe me, when you saw an Indian out on the plains settin' up on a pony with a Winchester in his hand or a lance, there was nothing poor about him. He was a fighting man from way back, and he was a savage... a stranger was an enemy, and an enemy was to be killed or, if captured, tortured to see how brave he was.

In my time I'd had my share of troubles with Comanches, Kiowas, Arapahos, Utes, Cheyennes, Sioux, and about every kind of redskin there was. With some I got along fine; but when he's fighting no Indian needs take a back seat for any man. They'd been called, by one of Europe's greatest generals, "the finest light cavalry under the sun."

When a man traveled in Indian country he sort of sifted through, gentle-like and taking up no more room than need be. He kept out of sight, and slept without a fire at night unless he could hide it well. And on top of that he prayed, if he was a praying man, and the deeper you got into Indian country the more of a praying man you got to be. You just couldn't afford to miss any bets.

Pio talked about the sheep. He talked about cattle. It would be no time at all, he was saying, until the Texas cattlemen started bringing their herds into the Panhandle. The buffalo was going, the Indian would be driven out, and the cattle would come.

"And then the farmers," I said, with disgust. My own folks had farmed, if you could call it that, on the thin soil of the Clinch Mountain slopes, but I wanted no farmers cutting up this country.

"No, this country is no good for farm," Pio said. "We try it. The wind blows too much. Only the grass ties it down."

"I know," I agreed, finishing off the last of the food on my plate. "That last dust storm we had, I could taste some Kansas dust in it. I knew a man one time in the Brazos country who could tell what county he was in by the taste of the dust."

Well, right then I made a big mistake. I looked over at that girl again. Of course, you've got to realize that I hadn't seen a white woman for a good long time, and this one was kind of special.

"All right, Pio," I said, "pick up the chips. You go tell them I'll try to get them through to Romero, anyway."

"*Bueno!*" Pio smiled at me. "I knew this was what you would do. I tell them so. I tell them just to wait, that you're a good man."

Me? It was the first time in a long while anybody had said that about Nolan Sackett. Oh, they say 'He's a good man with a gun,' or 'He's a fair hand with a rope,' or 'He can ride anything wears hair,' but nobody just out and said I was a good man.

A man had to avoid that sort of thing. First thing a man knows he's tryin' to live up to it. And then what kind of an outlaw is he?

So I glanced over there again and the girl smiled at me. Well, that was all right. And as for the breed, I always got along with breeds all right. Only that old man had too stiff a neck to suit me. He would be bull-headed as an old mossy-horn range cow.

Anyway, I was in for it. Least I could do was have another cup of coffee.

FIVE

Sitting at the table, I could look out the open door and into the street. The sun was bright on the street, but the doorway of the cantina was shadowed by huge old trees that stood nearby. Across the street were the cottonwoods and willows beyond which I had slept the night before.

It was pleasant, sitting there and looking out on that sunlit street, and I wished I had such a place of my own, a little cantina somewhere along a trail where folks would stop off from time to time. You never saw anything more peaceful.

On the other side of the street and down a bit, just where I could see just one window and a corner of a building, stood an adobe that was partly fallen to ruin. It was small, and was likely among the first houses built here.

Pio came back to my table with those three people, and they all sat down around the table, leaving me only a partial view out of the door.

"Señor Nolan Sackett," Pio said, "I wish you to meet Señor Jacob Loomis and Señorita Penelope Hume, and this here is Flinch."

Now, when I heard that name Hume I kept a straight face. My muscles never even twitched, me being a poker player of some experience. It seemed to me, all of a sudden, that the Llano Estacado was being invaded by folks all with the same idea.

"Howdy," I said, and just let it lay there. From now on until I got the lay of the land they could do the talking.

The man called Loomis spoke. "We understand you are riding toward Romero, and that you might guide us there. We would pay, of course."

Nobody had said anything about paying me until now, but for a man with no more money in his jeans than I was packing that was welcome news.

"It's risky," I said, knowing that committed me to nothing at all. "It's almighty risky. The Comanches and Kiowas are riding, and they're upset by the buffalo hunters coming south. You'd be better off to stay right where you are."

"In the middle of nowhere?" Loomis responded in a tone of disgust. "Young man, we'll give you fifty dollars to guide us, and to fight for us if there's trouble."

"For fifty dollars," I said, honestly enough, "I'd fight the whole Comanche tribe."

A flicker of shadow caught my eye, something in the background. Looking past Loomis, I could see nothing but the sunlight on the road and a lone hen pecking at something in the dust.

"Were you figuring on stopping in Romero?"

Now, I needn't have asked that question, because nobody stopped in Romero except the Mexicans who lived there. Romero was a nice, pleasant little place at the end of several trails, none of them traveled very much.

"We will decide about that when the time comes," he replied, and his voice was testy, as if he didn't care much for questions.

"All right," I said, "you be ready to pull out come day-break...and I mean first light, not a mite later."

"I will decide about that." Loomis was brusque. "You will get your orders from me."

"No," I said, "not if I am to take you through. If you want me for a guide, you'll go when I say, stop when I say, and make as little noise as ever you can." I got up. That shadow movement I'd seen was itching at me. "You make up your mind, Mr. Loomis. I am leaving out of here when there's a streak of gray in the sky. You want to go along, you all be ready, because that's when I'm going."

Oh, he didn't like it. He wasn't even one bit happy with me, and I didn't care. Fifty dollars was a lot of money, but a whole hide counted pretty high with me. Besides, I had a few dollars when I rode in, and I'd have most of it riding out.

Now, I hadn't missed the girl's name...Hume. And the man who supposedly hid that treasure in the Rabbit Ears was Nathan Hume. Some folks might consider that was just a coincidence, but not me.

Loomis pushed back from the table and was about to get up,

so I put my coffee cup down and said, "Seen some folks headed that way. City folks... young fellow and a girl."

You'd of thought I'd slapped him. "Didn't get their name," I said, "but the girl was called Sylvie. Matter of fact, there were three of them. I didn't cotton to 'em very much."

Penelope's eyes just got bigger and darker, it seemed like, but that old man went white as death. He sat down again, sat down hard, and for a minute or two he didn't say anything.

"You *saw* them?"

"Uh-huh... unpleasant folks, I'd say." I looked up at Loomis from under my eyebrows. "You know them?"

He said nothing for a moment, then shrugged. "Not with favor, sir, not with favor. A most untrustworthy lot."

He got up again. "Come, Penelope. Daybreak will come all too soon."

After they had gone I saw Pio watching me. "What is it, señor? Who are those people you spoke of? He was afraid of them, I think."

So I told him a little about Sylvie and her brother, enough to put him on his guard against them. "I'd say they were touched... off the trail somewhere in their heads, but what makes them dangerous is that they don't look it."

Whether he believed me I could not guess, but I left him to think about it and wandered outside. It was cool and pleasant under the old cottonwoods. The dun was living it up on that fresh green grass, with plenty of water close at hand. But I wasn't looking forward to playing shepherd to that buckboard.

With my back to a tree where I could look down the street, I considered what lay ahead... and kept an eye on that empty building across the street from the cantina. Had the flicker of movement come from there?

Time dragged slowly by, and I watched, half-dozing, yet my eyes were ready to catch any movement. Shadows fell around me, and I didn't think anybody could see me clearly—not to be sure, anyway. The dun was feeding right behind me, so nobody was going to come up on my blind side.

While I waited there I thought of tomorrow. Leaving town, we would go northwest along Punta de Aguas Creek, which emptied into the Canadian only a few miles off. Holding south of the creek, we could make Romero in three to four days, depending on how game they were to travel and how much trouble we had. With luck we could make ten, twelve miles in a day.

After a while I shifted the dun's picket pin to fresh grass, then, spurs jingling, strolled back to the cantina and sat down inside. Pio was gone, but the señora came out and brought me a meal of buffalo steak, eggs, and beans. I sat where I could keep an eye on the adobe on the other side of the street. When I'd been there only a few minutes, Penelope Hume came in.

Now, I'm no hand with womenfolks. I'm a rough, hardhanded man, doing most any kind of work or getting into any kind of a fighting shindig. Womenfolks, especially the young, pretty kind, put a loop on my tongue to where it can scarce wiggle. And this Penelope, she was fresh and lovely, and kind of sparkly when she laughed. Like I've said, she was a tall girl and well made. She was put together so that when she moved it had a way of making a man mighty restless.

"Mr. Sackett, may I sit down?"

Now there's things we don't know back in the Clinch Mountains, but a man knows enough to stand when a lady comes up to him, so I got up quick, almost spilling my coffee, and sat down only after she had been helped into her chair.

She looked across the table at me. "Mr. Sackett, I am glad you are going to show us the way to Romero, but I thought you should be warned. There's going to be trouble."

"I was born to it."

"I know. But you weren't born around Sylvie, Ralph, and Andrew."

"So you know them. Do they have another name?"

"Their name is Karnes. They are kinfolk, in a way...there's no blood relation between us. But they knew...well, they pried. They learned something only I was supposed to know; and now they are trying to get where we are going before we do."

I didn't ask any questions about that. The trouble was, these folks probably believed the secret of Nathan Hume's treasure was something only they knew. As far as the hiding place was concerned, if they knew that, it *was* something nobody else knew. But I was pretty sure I wasn't the only one who knew about that gold. Only most of the others didn't know as much as I did.

"What started you folks out here all to once?"

"My grandmother died, and when she died she mentioned a

packet of letters in her will, and they were to come to me, as my father and mother were both dead. Sylvie and Ralph were there, although they had no right to be. There was little enough to leave and, as I said, they were no blood relation. But they heard the reading of the will, and in it grandmother mentioned that in the packet of letters was an account of where Nathan Hume's gold was buried."

"Somebody must've got away and told about it. I mean, when Nathan Hume was killed."

"You knew about that?"

"He was a known man. He'd been taking pack trains from Missouri to Santa Fe for years."

"Grandfather drew a picture, wrote a few lines, and gave it to an Indian boy. He thought the boy might get away, and if he did he was to mail this to grandmother. The letter was all addressed, everything. Well, the Indian boy did get away, and he sent the message."

"How about Sylvie?"

"After the reading of the will she was just too nice, and so was Ralph. Sylvie made some tea—. What's the matter?"

"Sylvie offered me some coffee, one time."

"It may have been the same sort of thing. She made some tea, and I took it to my room, only I got busy writing letters and forgot to drink it. In the middle of the night I woke up and Sylvie was standing there reading the letters by candlelight.

"I got them away from her, but she was furious—she threatened me, laughed at me, said there was no gold, and even if there was I could never get it."

The sun had moved beyond the cottonwoods, throwing a shadow across the street and across our door. A dog trotted up the street and paused outside, and I watched him, for something worried him. He sniffed, trying to catch some scent that kept getting away from him.

It was a nice thing, setting here in this cool, pleasant room talking to Penelope Hume.

"You said your folks were dead. What about Loomis—who is he?"

"He was a friend of my father, and of my grandfather too. He offered to help. Flinch found us, or we found him, at Fort Griffin. He has been very loyal."

That answered one question for me. If I could answer the one about the adobe across the street I'd be happier, but I had a good idea about that, too. And I was watching the dog. He was a big dog, and part wolf by the look of him, with all a wolf's suspicion.

We talked of other things, Penelope and me. She told me of her home back in New York state, and I talked a bit about Tennessee, but more about the country we were in.

"Folks out here are a rough lot, ma'am. There's the good and the bad, and there's many a man who has come west to get away from something, some trouble he's had. You'll find men from the oldest families and with the best education working right alongside a cowhand who can't read or write.

"The trouble is, too many folks come just to get rich and then get out. They don't care what they leave behind as long as they can take riches with them."

All the time I talked I thought of how it seemed to set across the table from such a girl, me who owned nothing but a pistol, a Winchester, a beat-up blanket or two, and a borrowed horse. And likely would never have anything more.

"I'd better go," she said. "Mr. Loomis wouldn't like it at all if he knew where I was."

"You're all right with me," I said; "but ma'am, I'd not be trusting of folks. There are some would murder you for what you know about Nathan Hume."

"My dear cousins? I know."

"Not only them," I said. "When it comes to money or a pretty woman, there's not many who can be trusted."

"Not you, Mr. Sackett?"

"I've the name of being an outlaw," I said.

SIX

A spatter of rain was falling when Flinch led out the horses in the morning. It was dark, with only a faint suggestion of light showing beyond the cottonwoods. Underneath them it was still like night. I tethered the dun near the buckboard and, rifle in hand, went across to Pio's.

The room was lighted by candles. It was warm and pleasant, with the smell of breakfast cooking. Loomis was already at the table, his face stiff with sleep; only the eyes seemed awake. Drawing up a chair, I sat down opposite him, and was scarcely seated when Penelope came in, hurrying to her chair. I rose and seated her, and Loomis gave me a dark, angry look.

Whether he was irritated with me because he believed I was making up to her, I don't know, and cared less. Flinch came in, walking quiet as a ghost, and sat down at the end of the table.

The señora came from the kitchen with a platter of food, and then brought a steaming pot of coffee. We ate in silence, all of us heavy with sleep. As for me, I knew I should be thinking of the trail ahead, and the day before us. But I could not keep my thoughts from going back to yesterday, and the dog.

Whoever had been in the adobe house across the way had gone before the dog could find him. I remembered how the dog, hackles stiff, had walked toward the adobe, growling. Nobody else had seemed to be watching him.

He went inside the open doorway, and I got up and strolled across the street and followed him. He knew me, had been smelling around when I picketed my horse the night before, and had seen me that day around Pio's house. He looked up at me, then smelled around the empty room.

The lean-to behind the adobe showed where a man had slept and smoked cigarettes, a lot of them. The big dog sniffed curiously, then wandered out to the low back wall where the man had evidently gone. . . .

Steve Hooker? I wondered.

It was still dark when we went outside. The air was cool and the spatter of raindrops had begun again. The old buckboard creaked when they climbed into it. Flinch gathered the reins, and they moved off.

Pio came out as I stepped into the saddle. "I do not like it, *amigo*," he said. "The señorita will have trouble, I think. We like her very much, my wife and I."

"Her worst enemies are behind us. The ones of whom I spoke. Tell them nothing."

"*Adios*," he said, and I left him there, and moved out after the buckboard.

We crossed the Canadian, which was mostly a wide bed of sand, and then went west on the farther side, keeping well back from the bank to avoid the numerous creeks. But occasionally we traveled in the dry river bed itself, the narrow stream of the river shifting from one side to the other as we moved along. By daylight we were well on our way.

Riding ahead, I scouted the country for Indians or for anybody else who might be around. As it grew light, I swung right and left now and again to cut for sign. Most of the tracks I found were those of sheep from Borregos Plaza, or of buffalo.

The light rain increased, and I led the way out of the river bed. It never took long in this country for a flash flood to come, and I didn't know how much it had been raining up the country.

When we were maybe a mile back from the river, I caught movement in the willows ahead and below us, and two riders came in sight from the direction of the river. At that distance I couldn't make them out, but they never so much as glimpsed us, but rode on ahead.

It took only a few minutes for me to ride down the hill and pick up their sign. They had been bedded down under a rough shelter on the bank of the river overlooking the trail, and they had been waiting there for some time. Crouching, I looked back the way we had come. They must have seen us leave the river bed.

Who were these two who had been tricked out of their ambush by sheer luck? If there had not been those heavy clouds in the distance and that rain to worry me about the river bed, we would have walked into the ambush and they would have had us cold turkey.

Where they had waited they had a thick screen of boughs for concealment, and yet a perfect field of fire through neatly prepared openings in the brush where they had broken away leaves and twigs. They could have taken me and one of the others with the first two shots, and the ones who were left would never have gotten away.

Those two men were western men; I knew that by the way they rode, and they were experienced at their work. Right then I began casting around in my memory for some clue as to who they might be.

Men hired for the job, surely. I could bet on that. So who was there around Griffin or Fort Phantom Hill who might be hired?

The names I came up with weren't happy ones to think about. I knew of several around this part of the country, and any one of them would be a package of trouble. The two who had laid for us were good at their job, too good for comfort.

I walked the dun up out of the brush and across the green slope through the rain, and was thinking about what would happen when all of these treasure-seekers reached the Rabbit Ears at the same time... Or could we get there first?

"Who were those men?" Loomis asked as I came back to the buckboard.

He had had his eyes open then. "Hunters... big-game hunters, Mr. Loomis, and we're the game."

"They were waiting for us?" He was incredulous. "Who could they be?"

"Somebody hired for cash to do a job. Good at the work, too. We were lucky this time, but we can't count on luck next time. Mr. Loomis, I didn't figure on this when I signed up with you, but it looks like I've got to go hunting for them. Either I take those men, or they'll take us."

He didn't come up with any objection, and from his remarks he seemed more worried about who was doing the hiring than about the killers themselves. There was nothing I could tell him about that, but I knew we were in trouble a-plenty. The best way I knew to keep those two from doing their job was to find them first.

The rain continued to fall—a light, gentle rain. Although there was no flash flood in the river, the water widened and deepened, and we went on, keeping some distance back from the bank.

It was close to noontime before we turned off up Punta de Agua Creek. We had to pick our way along, avoiding obvious places of ambush and trying to keep in the open without becoming too good a target. It wasn't easy.

My dun covered twice the distance of that buckboard, just checking back and forth. We held north on the right of the creek and when we made camp on Los Redos Creek we were about half a mile back of its junction with Punta de Agua.

Nobody had much to say. All of us were beat from the rough country we'd crossed, and Loomis was glum and mean looking. We watered the horses, then picketed them in close. I put together a bed for Penelope, and then went out a ways from camp and bedded down near a rock wall where nobody could come up on me sudden, and where I had a lookout over the camp.

The trend of Punta de Agua was a little westward, then north, but when we started out again we held due north. About four miles out the creek turned westward, but I kept the buckboard headed north. I had a hunch that would worry those men who were packing guns for us, for if we were headed for the Rabbit Ears and Romero it would seem more than likely that we would follow the creek. However, Punta de Agua Creek took another bend north, and I figured to cut west and pick up the creek at that bend.

I rode ahead and scouted the country and we made good time. The rain had stopped, but the slopes were wet and slippery. Meanwhile, I was doing some contemplating. Those ambushers would be somewhere ahead...but where? If I could figure that out, I might sort of roust around and get the best of them.

We turned suddenly and headed due west for Rita Blanca Creek, and when we reached it we stopped to eat. Loomis was giving me angry looks and he stalked off to the crest of a rise.

"He'll get himself killed if he isn't careful," I said to Penelope, who was standing near me.

But I wasn't watching Loomis, I was watching Flinch. The

breed had me puzzled. He was a canny man, and a quiet one who did no talking at all, but he didn't seem to miss much. A couple of times I'd seen him casting about for sign. Now he was gathering sticks for a fire.

There was a good bit of broken brush and dead stuff lying near the creek. Flinch moved like a wild animal. A wild creature will move through the forest and never step on a fallen twig or branch. A horse might, or a cow, but never a deer or other wild animal, and Flinch was like that. You just never heard him as he moved, and scarcely saw him.

Was it entirely coincidence that he had been around when Loomis was looking for somebody to join them? He had not said he was familiar with this country, but I was sure he knew it as well if not better than I did myself.

As Penelope and I were talking, Loomis came back, and he looked at her sharply. "Penelope! You come here!"

She turned, her chin up. "Mr. Loomis, I will not have you speaking to me like that! You're not my father, and you're not my guardian!"

A moment there he was mad enough to strike her had she been close enough. He glared at her, then said stiffly, "I gave up my business to come and help you. Is this the thanks I get?"

Well, I had to hand it to her, the way she stood up to him. "Mr. Loomis, I am very grateful for your coming, and I thank you for it, but that gives you no right to direct my life. If we find the gold, you will be paid."

At that, his face flushed. "You talk too much!" he flared.

"If you mean she talks too much about Nathan Hume's gold," I said casually, "you're wrong. She's never mentioned it until now, and as far as that goes, nearly everybody in this here country knows that story. I'd bet a pretty penny Flinch knows it, too." I looked at Flinch.

He looked back at me and said nothing, but he knew all right.

"Her name was enough, even if it hadn't been for other things."

Now, I'd lied a little bit there, saying she'd said nothing about the gold, but she was in trouble enough and I wanted to leave Loomis without a leg to stand on. And I was beginning to be suspicious of his motives. He didn't strike me as the sort to pull up stakes and take a young girl west on a wild gold chase.

"This ain't exactly a traveled country," I added, "and the route you're takin' ain't the one I'd have picked for you. But I'll take you through to Romero if that's where you want to go. Or if it suits you better, I'll take you right to the Rabbit Ears."

Penelope looked thoughtful. "Which is the shortest?"

"Right up Rita Blanca Creek, I'd say. The difference is slight, but it *is* a difference, and the travel is a whole lot easier."

"We have to go to Romero," Loomis said stubbornly. "I planned on buying supplies there."

"If you know where the gold is," I suggested, "you'd be better off to get there as fast as you can and get it before the whole country moves in on you.

"Somebody paid those gents who were laying out for you. Maybe it was that Karnes outfit, maybe somebody else. I'd suggest you move fast and get there first...if you can."

Well, that slowed him down. He wanted that gold, and he wanted it almighty bad. After a moment he said, "All right, you take us the quickest way."

We headed off the way we'd been traveling. This was a wide-open and barren country, but there were long swells you'd scarcely call hills that would offer some concealment. I knew how to cross country unseen, for I was a man who'd lived that way.

Riding warily, I studied the country around, and suddenly came upon a stretch of rock swept clean by the wind. It was a place where there was a little firewood from dead brush on the creek banks, so we pulled up and made camp. It was early, but I had an idea of what I wanted to do.

We made a small fire and boiled some coffee and ate supper. I cleared a space around the fire so it wouldn't spread. Then I added some sticks that would burn slowly and would add more fuel to the fire kind of gradual. I even built a small rack of sticks above the fire, with the stick ends right in the flames. This would in time drop down, and help to keep the fire going.

When it was full dark I pulled my people back into the darkness. I wrapped the trace chains so they wouldn't jangle, and then we took off into the night, leaving the fire burning behind us. I knew that fire, rigged the way it was, would keep burning or smoking until well after daylight, and by that time I figured to be well away. We pulled out across the rock, and then into the scattered dunes. Those dunes by day were always feathered with a little wind-blown sand, and whatever tracks we made wouldn't last long.

This was bunch-grass country with ridges or dunes or sand breaking through from time to time. We headed north, keeping away from the creek but riding parallel to it. We traveled well into the night, and it was after midnight when we came to the place I was hunting, a sort of slough with cattails around it, in a hollow among the low hills. We pulled up there, to spend the rest of the night there without a fire.

I slipped on my moccasins, and went out and dusted over our last tracks a mite. Then I taken my own horse and went down into the cattails to a place I knew where there was a piece of solid ground among them, and there I staked out my horse and bedded down, maybe a hundred feet or so off from the others. Nobody could get to me without splashing into water, and the dun would let me know anyway. Then I slept, not worrying about a knife in the ribs or a knock on the skull.

There was a time there before I slept when I lay thinking back over the past few days, but thinking ahead. It was in my mind to try to foresee what might happen, and so be prepared for it. There's no way I know of that a body can foresee the future, but sometimes he can read it pretty well if he knows the way folks think.

Now, there's something about gold and the finding of it that changes a man's viewpoint. When it came to gold, I trusted nobody, not even myself. I'd never had much, and the sight of all that gold might turn me into a worse man than I figured to be.

Moreover, it might affect the others, and I'd no amount of respect for any of them, unless it was the girl. A young girl alone in the world without money is in for a hard time. She's prey to all sorts of advances and misfortunes, and hers can be a hard-bought life. Whatever happened, I wanted to see that the girl got her share of it.

I was thinking of myself too. Where there was gold I figured to get my share of it; but I had an idea that when that gold was found it would be every man for himself and the devil take the hindmost.

Morning came too soon and I was scarce awake, it being something short of daylight, when I heard a faint rustle in the water. I opened my eyes and looked up at the dun and his ears were pricked, so I just naturally reached down beside me and laid hand to my old Tinker.

Now, a Tinker-made knife was a handsome thing with a cutting edge like a razor—I often shaved with mine—but a strong blade that would cut through bone as well as flesh. They were made by a traveling peddler and tinker from back in the mountains, a gypsy man who traveled through, selling other things too, but from time to time with a Tinker-made knife to sell.

The water rustled, just faintly, and I thought of how a body approached this island in the reeds, and how much could be seen before he got right on it. Suddenly I heard the squish of a wet boot and looked up to see Loomis standing there with an axe in his hand.

He was within reach of me, and he had that axe ready, but when our eyes met he stopped. His eyes were as mean-looking as I've ever seen. Now, I've lived a good part of my life in difficulties, and my mind thinks in terms of fighting. The way he was holding that axe told me he was going to cut down and to the left with it. A man swinging an axe from the right-shoulder side can't cut much to the right. Not with accuracy.

Loomis, if he tried to hit me, would cut down and left, so I was all braced to roll right and come up. His knuckles were white with gripping the axe, and I could see the hate in his face. Of a sudden it came to me that, old as he was, Loomis didn't only want that gold, he wanted the girl.

A moment there I thought he was stopped, then he suddenly took a deep, rasping breath and swung. The breath warned me, but he swung faster than I'd thought and I just skinned by, the axe missing by inches.

But then I was on my feet, like a cat, and had my Tinker pointed tight against his wishbone. He didn't have a chance to lift that axe again; my knife was right where I could open him up, and he knew it. I looked right down into his eyes and said, "Loomis, you're a murdering skunk. I got me a notion to kill you."

All the same I was in a fix, and I knew it. If he killed me, nobody would question it much. Penelope might, but she would have nobody to argue with, and I was a known outlaw. Flinch would say nothing of it, or think nothing of it. On the other hand, if I killed him, nobody would believe me at all.

So I just looked into his eyes . . . we stood chest to chest, not eighteen inches between us, and I reached up with my knife and flicked a button from his coat...and then another, and another, until I was right under his chin. Then I touched the point under his chin and just pricked him a mite.

"Mr. Loomis," I said, "you hadn't ought to done that. You make a body right mistrustful of folks. Now you just turn your tail around and hike back to camp...And, Mr. Loomis, don't you ever try that again or I'll part your brisket with this blade."

Well, he was sweating like nothing you ever saw, he was that scared. He backed off, and then turned and ran back through the water.

I saddled up and loaded up and, taking my Winchester, walked the dun along the edge of the slough for a ways, then came out and skirted the camp. I wanted to scout the country anyway, but I also wanted to come into camp so's I could see everybody. It wasn't in my mind to ride up and have somebody a-laying for me.

When I rode in Penelope gave me an odd look, but nothing was said. I had an idea Flinch knew what was going on, for that breed missed very little. He was the sort that remains on the side lines and then picks up the pieces after the fighting is over.

We took out across the prairie. They would be hunting us by now, and no doubt would be following along streams where there was water. But from now on there were a good many scattered sloughs or pools, and water would not be so hard to come by.

That night we made camp in a depression north of Carrizo Creek, a place unlikely to be seen until a man was within a few yards of it.

Loomis was restless and on edge. He avoided me, and I was just as glad. Squatting near the fire, I drank hot black coffee and talked to Penelope. It had been a while since I'd had a chance to talk to any girl.

"You be careful," I warned her there at the last; "you trust nobody. You're a mighty pretty girl, and where gold and women are concerned not many can be trusted."

"How about you, Nolan?" This was the first time she had called me by my given name.

"Me neither. I'm as hungry for gold as the next man."

"And women?"

"Well, up to a point. My ma raised me to respect womenfolks."

She was quiet for a minute or two and then she spoke very quietly. "I don't trust people altogether, Nolan."

"You must trust Loomis, to come clear out here with him."

"He's old enough to be my father. Or my grandfather, almost. Besides, how else could I get out here? Would you tell someone how to find a buried treasure and just let them go, hoping you'd get a share?"

"Nope."

"Neither would I."

We moved out from camp before the first light. There were clumps of mesquite about, and more prickly pear than we had been seeing before. I shucked my Winchester and rode with it to hand. We angled northwest across the country, headed for a crossing of Perico Creek almost due south of the Rabbit Ears.

The dun and me, we stayed off to one side, either in front of the buckboard or behind it, always keeping it within sight; but I was careful to offer no target for my back.

Where, I wondered, was Sylvie Karnes and her brothers? And what had become of Steve Hooker?

Topping out on a low rise I saw the Rabbit Ears off to the north, showing just above the horizon and a good ways off. They were two nubbins of mountain, scarcely big enough to be called a mountain in this country. But even from this distance you could see why it got its name of Rabbit Ears.

It was near noontime, and we were a mile or so short of the ford. Down off the rise you couldn't see the Rabbit Ears, and I said nothing about them to the others.

The thought in my mind was that we were now within a few miles of more gold than most people had ever seen, and unless I missed my guess half a dozen people were ready to kill for it.

A moment there I thought, why not just light out? Why walk into something that was none of my business? Let the murdering Karnes outfit and the rest of them fight it out... was any amount of gold worth that much risk? I doubted it.

It would be mighty easy to turn my horse and ride away. A few days' ride to the west was Mora, where I had kinfolk. To the north there were the hell-for-leather mining towns where a man could make do one way or another. A twitch of the bridle and I would be off and free-riding with nothing to worry about but Comanches.

The trouble was, there was a girl back there; and mean though I might be, I couldn't leave that girl to a pack of wolves. It just wasn't in me.

Every ounce of horse sense I had told me to cut and run, but I swung my horse and rode on toward the ford on the Perico.

And right into a bellyful of trouble.

SEVEN

Steve Hooker, Tex Parker, and Charlie Hurst were sitting their horses just across the ford, blocking the trail. They all had rifles, and they were just sitting there, and Hooker was grinning. The thing was, they expected me to stop.

"You boys want something?" I called out.

"You turn around and git out'n here!" Hurst yelled. By that time I was at the water's edge.

That water was no more than eight inches deep and there was good hard bottom, so I let the dun have the spurs and went through the water and up the bank and into them before they realized I wasn't going to stop and parley.

They sure enough expected me to pull up and talk about it, but when trouble faces me I never was much on the talk. So I rode right into them, and then I dropped the reins and slammed right and left with the rifle.

Hurst tried to duck, but the rifle barrel caught him behind the ear and knocked him from the saddle. Parker was reaching for me when I swung the rifle across and drove the barrel into the side of his head. It struck with a *tunk* like the butt of an axe against a log, and he went out. Grabbing the reins as my horse turned, I put the muzzle of the gun on Steve Hooker. His own rifle was coming up and I shot him, holding high a-purpose so he'd take it through the shoulder. He jerked, but stayed in the saddle, losing his grip on his rifle.

He started to swear, and I said, "You still got a left hand. You want to try for none?"

"You played hell!" he shouted at me. "Do you know who those boys are?"

"Sure. They ride with Bill Coe. I know all that outfit, and you can tell Coe he knows where I am if he ever wants to come hunting."

55

"You think he won't?"

"That's right. I know Coe, and he knows me. You'd have to weigh a lot of gold in the other side of the scales before he'd make a move toward me."

The buckboard came down to the water and drew up sharply. "What's going on here?" Loomis called.

"No trouble," I said, and swinging down I caught Parker by the scruff of the neck and dragged him clear of the trail. Both of their horses had been frightened into running off a ways. "Drive right on through. These boys figured to stop us, but they had a change of mind."

Penelope's face was white and shocked. "Are . . . are those men dead?"

"No, ma'am. They'll both have headaches tomorrow, that's all."

"Was this necessary?" Loomis demanded.

"If you want to cross the ford it was necessary. You wanted me to take you where you're going and I'm doing it."

Wheeling the dun, I rode off up the trail, and the buckboard rattled on after me. It didn't make a mite of difference what Loomis thought, but the expression on Penelope's face bothered me. A lot of people hear about violence but never come face to face with it, and they've no experience with men of violence. One thing I'd learned a long time back: you just can't waste time talking. If there's talking to do, do it afterwards.

All the time we'd been traveling I'd been looking for wagon tracks. I didn't see how the Karnes outfit—Sylvie, Ralph, and Andrew—could make it faster than we had, but it never pays to weigh an opponent too light.

It was a far-stretching open land through which we rode. It was a country with lava outcroppings here and there, with the yellow-brown grass and the green showing through. It was the bright green of mesquite, and the oddly jointed clumps of prickly pear. A man could hear the cicadas singing endlessly in the brush, and from time to time he'd see a rattler curled in the shade of a bush.

It was bunch-grass country where buffalo ran, and it was mustang country, wild and free. Maybe I would never have very much in the way of money, but I'd have the memories of this land when it was fresh and open, the memories of one of the grandest pieces of country a man could ever see.

The dun liked it, too. Whenever we topped out on a rise his nostrils would widen to test the wind, and he'd toss his head a little, ears pricked, looking straight away into the far distance.

Well, we were a part of this country, that dun mustang and me. Our natures bred us for it, and our way of living was the way the country demanded.

Back there I'd mentioned William Coe. Now, I would never hold him as a small-calibered man. Coe had a gang of men and a stone fortress not far north of here on the Cimarron, a regular Robbers' Roost. His men were tough and wild and uncurried. He was a steady man, if an outlaw, not one to be stampeded into doing anything foolish. I wasn't hunting trouble with Coe, and he wouldn't be hunting any with me... unless the price was right.

But if we got that gold out of the ground—three hundred pounds of it—the price would be right and all bets off. But Coe wasn't going to come hunting my kind of trouble because I'd rough-handled some of his men. He'd figure they were big boys now, big enough to saddle their own broncs.

Coe knew me maybe as well as I knew myself, for we'd been acquainted back yonder. He knew that trouble had become blood-kin to me, and that something in me wouldn't let me back up or back down, no matter what happened. When trouble showed, when I was faced with it, I just naturally stiffened my neck and went ahead. There was a streak of wildness in me, a streak of recklessness that I disliked. The cool way was the best way, that I knew, but at times I just naturally went hog-wild and started throwing lead or punches at whatever was in the way. It was going to get me killed some day.

The Rabbit Ears were standing up there plain now. I could see them clear, and so could Loomis and the others, so I dropped back alongside the buckboard.

"There they are, Loomis," I said, "and whatever happens will happen soon now. If we can get in there first and get that gold out, and high-tail it out of here, we may get away without a fight. But we won't have much time."

"How much time do we have?"

"Maybe a day... maybe a day and a night. No longer."

"Do you think Hooker rounded up those men himself? Or were they acting for somebody else?"

"I think it was his show, but from here on it may not be. Those other men were outlaws of the Coe gang...their Roost isn't far from here. If Coe gets wind of that gold, and we get it out of the ground, we'll have us a running fight."

"Does he have many men?"

"Anywhere from three to thirty, depending on who is hanging out up there. He will have enough."

Now I dropped behind them and stayed off to one side. As we rode I studied the country, cutting for sign. There had been some movement around, and it worried me. Rabbit Ears Mountain wasn't far off the Santa Fe Trail, but as a usual thing there wasn't too much movement off the trail. But now there had been.

I was a fool to go riding over there for a treasure of which I'd been offered no part, guiding them there, and then having to choose whether or not to leave Penelope to her friends and her enemies, or to stay on and fight and perhaps get no thanks in the end.

But she was a fair lady, a girl's bright eyes have won the day more than once, and I was the fool ever to look into them. For I am an unhandsome man, and the romance in my heart does not show past the bend in my nose, or at least the girls don't seem to look beyond that.

Back in our Tennessee hills we had few books to read, and I'd never learned beyond the spelling out of words; but we had copies of Sir Walter Scott there in the mountains, and a teacher or a preacher to read them to us in passing. It was always as Ivanhoe that I saw myself, and always as the Norman knight that I was being seen by others.

Yet being the fool I was, I was forever riding into trouble because of a pair of pretty lips or a soft expression in the eyes of a girl. Nor was this time to be different. Even as I thought of riding off into the night, I knew it was not in me to go, and I'd risk a bullet in the back from that cold chill of a man up yonder in the buckboard. Or maybe from that quiet one who sat saying nothing, but seeing and hearing everything, that Flinch, who was one to fear and be careful of.

The Rabbit Ears were close now, so I closed in on the buckboard. My foolishness for the eyes of Penelope did not lead me to foolishness with Loomis. There was no nonsense in me where men were concerned, and if he wanted my kind of trouble I'd serve it up hot and well done for him, and he'd get indigestion from it, too, or I'd know the reason why.

"There are the Rabbit Ears," I said. "No doubt you know where to find the gold of Nathan Hume."

Loomis drew up, for he was driving then, and he reached in his pocket and paid me fifty dollars.

"Your money," he said. "You've been paid, and we have no more use for you."

Penelope was keeping her eyes straight front, so I said to her, "And you, ma'am? If you want me to stay and see you clear with your gold, I'll do it, and no pay asked or wanted."

"No," she said, not looking at me at all. "No, I want nothing more from you. Mr. Loomis is here. He will take care of things."

"I've no doubt," I said, and turned my horse away, but not my eyes, for I knew Loomis was one to shoot a man in the back if chance offered. At the moment, I almost wished he would take the chance, so that I might lay him dead across the buckboard seat.

I skirted a low hill and drew up in the shade of a clump of mesquite to contemplate.

This was another time when the maiden fair saw me only as the Norman knight.

EIGHT

So I'd been given my walking papers, and now there was nothing to keep me here. Penelope Hume had said not a word to keep me, and I was no longer responsible. Moreover, this was not the kind of country I cottoned to, wishing more for the sight of trees and real mountains right now, although I'll say no word against the far-reaching plains, wherever they lie.

The Rabbit Ears were basaltic rock—or lava, if that comes easier. There were ancient volcanoes to the north, and much of this country had been torn and ruptured by volcanic fires long ago. Where the wind had swept the flat country clear it was sandstone.

The Rabbit Ears could scarcely be called a mountain, as I've said. They were more like big mounds, falling away on all sides. At their highest they stood about a thousand feet above the surrounding country.

Circling wide, I drifted on across country to the north and watered at Rabbit Ears Creek, then followed the creek toward the west. On the northwest side of the mountain I found myself a notch in the rocks screened by brush and low trees, where there was a patch of grass sub-irrigated by flow from the mountain.

I staked the dun out on the grass and, swapping boots for moccasins, I climbed up the mountain. It was sundown, with the last rays of the sun slanting across the land and showing all the hollows.

There was a thin line of smoke rising from the brush along Rabbit Ears Creek; more than likely this was the camp of Loomis, Penelope, and Flinch.

Over east, maybe seven or eight miles from there, I caught a suggestion of smoke, and near it a white spot. It was so far off that had the sun not picked up that white I might never have noticed

it. Even the smoke might be something my expectation had put
there after I glimpsed that spot of white. For that white could be
nothing but a wagon top... the Karnes outfit, or somebody else.

What about Hooker? He had a bad shoulder. Tex and Charlie
Hurst would have aching heads. Would they quit now? I decided
it was unlikely.

William Coe would be at his Roost over on the Cimarron, not
nearly as far away as I wished, for his was a tough, salty outfit, and
Coe was game. He'd fight anything at the drop of a hat; he'd even
drop it himself.

His outfit had raided Trinidad, had even raided as far east as
Dodge, and had stolen stock from Fort Union, government stock.
They had nerve. If one of those boys rode for Coe, I'd be in trouble.

On the north side of Rabbit Ears all the ravines ran down
toward Cienequilla Creek. The location of the box canyon was
unknown to me, and it might be anywhere between the mountain
and the creek, or even over on the other side.

After I'd walked and slid back down the mountain I shifted
the dun's picket-pin to fresh grazing and made myself a pot of
coffee from dry, relatively smokeless wood. In the corner where I
was the fire couldn't be seen fifteen feet away.

A man on the dodge, or in Indian country, soon learns to
watch for such a place as this. His life depends on it. And if he
travels very much his memory is soon filled with such places. As
mine was.

Sitting beside the fire, I cleaned my pistol, my Winchester
lying at hand, just in case. Then I checked both of my knives. The
one I wore down the back of my neck inside my shirt collar slid
easy and nice from its scabbard. A time or two in passing through
brush or under low trees I'd gotten leaves or bits of them into the
scabbard, and I knew that in the next few days I might need that
knife almighty bad.

Later, lying on my blankets, I looked up at the stars through
the leaves. My fire was down to red coals and my pot was still full
of coffee. Tired as I was, I was in no mind to sleep.

My ears began making a check on all the little sounds around
me. They were sounds of birds, of insects, or of night-prowling
animals, and were familiar to me. But in every place some of the
sounds are different. Dead branches make a rattle of their own;

grass or leaves rustle in a certain way, yet in no two places are the sounds exactly the same. Always before I slept I checked the sounds in my mind. It was a trick I'd learned from an old Mexican sheep-herder and mountain man.

Of course the dun was there, and as I've said, there's nothing like a mustang to warn a man if he hears something strange. For that matter, I was of the same breed. I was a mustang man—a man riding the long prairie, the high mesa, the lonely ridges.

That Penelope now...

This was no time to think of her. Forcing my thoughts away from her, I considered the situation. Sylvie Karnes and her brothers wanted that gold, and they would stop at nothing to get it. I'd never come across anybody quite like them, and they worried me. I'd known plenty of folks who would kill for money, for hatred, or for a lot of reasons, but I'd met nobody so willing to kill just to be killing as they were, or appeared to be.

Sure as shootin', that coffee she fixed for me had been poisoned. No telling how many dead lay behind them, or lay ahead, for that matter.

Loomis would be after that gold, but he wanted the girl too. He would need her until they got the gold and after that? That was when Penelope Hume would come face to face with a show-down, and all alone.

Had she really wanted to go on without me? Or had they forced her to get rid of me? She had not looked my way even once, there at the end. Maybe they had talked her into it, but it might be that Loomis had threatened her.

Law and order were made for women. They are hedged around by protection. But out in the wilderness they are only as safe as men will let them be. Penelope Hume was a long way from any law, and it was likely that nobody even knew where she was, or where she was going. Loomis would have seen to that. If she never appeared again, nobody would be asking questions; and if anyone did ask, no one would answer. Many a man and many a woman disappeared in the western lands, left in an unmarked grave, or in no grave at all.

Whatever law there might be would be local law, administered only in the towns. Few officers ever rode out into the unsettled country unless they were Federal officers, and most of those were active only in the Indian Territory.

These were my thoughts as I mounted up and worked my way on down the mountain, keeping to whatever cover I could find. That box canyon would not be easy to find, but should be simpler for me, who knew this kind of country, than for either Loomis or the Karnes outfit.

Suppose I could get there first and get that gold out? Finders was keepers, wasn't that so? That was how I felt, and yet the idea made me uneasy. There would be nothing for that girl, for Penelope. I wasn't worried about Sylvie... her kind could always get along. Penelope was something else, and I couldn't leave her without a two-bit piece to her name.

She was pretty, and she was a city girl. Both qualities put her in a bad spot. She was pretty enough to attract trouble, and had too much of the city in her to know how to cope with this kind of country.

Right beyond me was a place where the canyon down which I was riding sort of opened out. There were trees along the creek ahead, and trees and brush along the mountainside. Slowing down, I peered ahead, searching for any sign of movement. I'd slip down there, I thought, find that box canyon, find the gold if I could, and then round up Penelope and the others and get the girl out of trouble.

It seemed to me she was safe until they either found or failed to find the gold; after that she would be fair game. Only I was uneasy, leaving her at all. She needed somebody at hand to care for her.

Ahead of me was some low brush; on the side of the mountain a few piñon. I started to swing around a big boulder when the corner of my eye caught a flash of light and I ducked. Something hit me a wicked blow on the skull, and the dun shied violently. A report went racketing off down the canyon, followed closely by another, and then I was laying on the ground among some rocks, looking at a pool of red on the sand.

Instinct told me I must move from where I lay, and yet I couldn't move a muscle. My brain told me to get up and get going, but nothing happened; and then I heard a voice call out.

"Ralph! You stop right there! I always was a better shot than you, and if you take one step nearer I'll break your leg!"

"Pen! Now, don't be foolish! We just came to help you. If you knew what we know about Loomis—"

"I don't need any help. You just turn back and leave that man alone."

"But he's after the gold, too! We've got to be rid of him, Pen!"

"You back up, Ralph! You and Sylvie and Andrew might just as well go home. You don't know where the gold is, and you'll never find it unless you know."

Ralph laughed, and it was an unpleasant laugh. "We don't have to find it, Pen. We'll just let you and Loomis do that for us!"

"You heard me, Ralph. Back up and let him alone."

"I'm going to kill him, Pen. If he isn't dead already, I'm going to kill him."

"Ralph"—Pen spoke matter-of-factly—"you make the slightest move this way and I'll not stop with breaking one leg—I'll break them both and just let you lie there. Nobody would ever find you except the buzzards."

Ralph must have believed her. I didn't see how he could, but maybe he knew her better than I did.

All that time, I simply couldn't move. I was all sprawled out among the rocks, and I seemed to be paralyzed. I could hear, all right, and I could see, but I couldn't move. But all the while I knew that if that girl had not stood there with a rifle, Ralph Karnes would have killed me.

After a bit, Penelope spoke, just loud enough for me to hear. "Mr. Sackett? Are you all right?"

Well, now, that was a foolish question. Did she figure that I'd be just a-lyin' here if I was all right? I tried to speak, and finally made a kind of weak sound. Then I tried to move. I made a real effort, and I felt a sort of spasm go through me, but nothing else happened.

Then I heard her coming. At least, I hoped it was her.

She came down over the rocks as if she was born to them, and she kept looking around to see if anybody was closing in on her. Then she was standing near me and looking down, and I looked right into her eyes.

"You're alive then," she said, and then she kind of bent down close to me. "We can't stay here," she said. "He'll be back with the others. He knows you're hurt."

She pulled my arm across her shoulder and tried to pull me up, but she wasn't strong enough.

My lips worked, and finally I managed to shape words. "Horse...get my horse."

She got up quickly, and as quickly was gone.

Meantime I tried to move my head, and managed it, then wrapped my fingers around a rock and tugged. The rock held, and I moved myself a little. With care, I managed to work that hand up the side of a slab of rock, but I had no strength at all in it, and it fell back to my side. I couldn't seem to make my fingers work as they should, and my head was starting to ache with a dull, heavy throb. I didn't think I was seriously hurt. Maybe I just didn't dare think so, for to be badly hurt here was almost the same as being dead; yet I had been shot, hit in the head, it seemed, and had been temporarily shocked into some kind of paralysis.

To a man who has spent his life depending on his muscles and his reflexes, there could be nothing more frightening than the state I seemed to be in now. I'd made my living with strength, and with my skill in any kind of shooting, and without that, I had nothing. I'd never had no chance for schooling, and if I couldn't count on my muscles there'd be nothing left for me.

I found I could work the fingers of the other hand like a claw, opening and closing them. I got my hand on an edge of rock and tugged myself up, one-handed, to a kneeling position.

I knew I had to get out of here. Those murdering Karneses would be coming a-hunting me. If I was dead they'd be wanting to see the body; and if I wasn't, they had to know it and finish me off.

Penelope was coming back, leading the dun. I was surprised he had let her come up to him, he was that shy of strangers. But that girl had a way about her...and nerve too.

When the dun came alongside me he snorted nervously, smelling blood, which was trickling down my face now. I spoke softly to him. "Easy, boy, easy now."

With my one working hand I reached out and caught hold of the stirrup leather. Penelope slipped her arm around my waist, and with her lifting and my grip on the stirrup I managed to pull myself erect. But when the horse took a step, I almost went to the ground; it was only Penelope's tight grip that held me up.

We started to move off, my feet trying to work but dragging. We hadn't made more than twenty feet before Penelope, glancing over her shoulder, let go of me, and I grabbed wildly with my one good hand to hang onto the stirrup.

Her rifle went to her shoulder and she fired in the same instant. Then she fired again. The dun was still walking dragging me toward the brush.

"Go, boy, go!" I said to him, and he went.

A shot came from somewhere and a bullet hit sand near me. Another shot, and it struck somewhere above me and the dun jumped, but I hung on until we got into a clump of juniper. Then I let go, and fell face down in the sand.

Penelope shot once more, and then I heard her scrambling in the rocks. After that silence.

The dun had stopped among the trees, nostrils wide. My face was wet with blood and sweat, and I was trembling all over. My Winchester was in the boot, but I couldn't reach it.

Had Penelope been shot? Everything was so quiet. The sun was hot. I could smell dust and blood and sweat. Reaching back, I got the thong off my Colt and fished it out and up where I could shoot.

Nothing moved, and there was not a sound. The dun switched his tail, nosed at some brush, then pricked his ears to listen. Struggling, I managed to lift my head. All I could see was roots and rock. Underneath me there was blood on the sand, my blood.

What had happened to Penelope? And where was Loomis? For some reason I hadn't given a thought to him, nor to Flinch.

It was the Karneses who worried me. It must have been the Karneses shooting. And where was Steve Hooker and his outfit? For they must have heard the shooting if they were anywhere within miles, for sound carried on those wide plains.

Reaching out, I caught my fingers over a root and tugged myself closer to the trunk of a tree. It was a mighty slim tree, but I was in no position to argue about cover.

The worst of it was, I couldn't see a thing. I had cover of a sort, but I couldn't even see if anybody was moving out there.

Was Penelope alive? Was she hurt? I'd no way of moving to find out—all I could do was lie there and wait, gun in hand.

The dun stamped his feet. Somewhere a pebble rattled. I shifted my gun and wiped my palm dry on my shirt. After a minute I put the gun down on a piece of bark and started to knead the muscles of the other arm, trying to get some life into it. My head ached heavily, but the bleeding seemed to have stopped. Presently I took up the gun again, fearing to risk any more time with it out of my hand.

The throbbing in my head had me wrinkling my brow against it, and my throat was dry, needing water. There was water in the creek, and in my canteen on the saddle, but one seemed as far off as the other.

Reaching out now, I gripped the trunk of the tree and pulled myself further along. It was much too quiet out there, and I was scared for Penelope.

Looking out over the low brush and rocks, I searched for her, but could see no sign of her. I looked across the mouth of the canyon, and let my eyes move slowly across the rocky wall and the scattered boulders at the canyon's mouth, then down on the tree-dotted flatland that sloped away toward the creek.

Nothing...

And then behind me I heard a faint movement. Turning my head, I looked across the small clearing among the trees and brush. The dun was standing head up, nostrils wide, looking toward my right. Stiffly, I turned my head.

Andrew was standing very still in a narrow space between two clumps of mesquite, a prickly pear almost waist-high in front of him. He was holding his rifle up, ready to shoot, and his eyes were moving along the thicker brush on my side, looking for me.

And when he shot, he would shoot to kill.

NINE

Andrew Karnes was no more than sixty feet away, but I was drawn back under the low-growing juniper and it was not easy to see me. His eyes were shifting around quickly, like a weasel's eyes, hunting something to kill.

My pistol was in my right hand, and I was looking back over my left shoulder. To shoot, I'd have to swing around, and that would make a noise. I had watched Andrew, and I knew he was quick as a cat—and there was no way I could move without giving him the first shot. I didn't want to chance it at that range. So I just lay there, hoping he wouldn't see me.

He came forward a step. His eyes went to the horse again, then began again their restless search for me.

I was going to risk it. I would have to. When his eyes got down to the farthest rocks, I would roll over and fire. I wouldn't be in the best shooting position, but I had no choice. It was him or me.

The dun stomped his hoof, and Andrew looked in that direction. Not wanting to take my eyes from him, I moved my left hand to a position under my left shoulder and pushed up, then I moved my right arm under my body.

Actually, I hadn't an idea whether I could do it. Each movement was a gamble, and each might be my last. My left hand started across my body. My eyes were on Andrew; my right hand was coming forward... and then he saw me.

He must have failed to believe what he saw. Or maybe the shadows were thick enough so what he saw was indistinct, for there was an instant when he froze. And then the rifle whipped to his shoulder.

Even as he moved, I moved; my left hand slapped the ground and my right thrust forward. My gun must have gone off an instant sooner, or perhaps he shot too fast, for the bullet *whapped* into the ground right where my body had been before the half-turn was completed.

My own shot was high. It cut a furrow across the top of his shoulder and his involuntary move jerked the rifle out of line. He levered another bullet into the chamber, but my second shot went right through his face. It was a miss, for I'd shot at his body, but the bullet went in under his eye and came out the back of his head.

He fell forward, all sprawled out, into that mess of prickly pear. The rifle, thrown forward as he fell, dropped into the sand beyond the patch of cactus. I held the gun on him, ready for another shot, even after I realized the back of his skull was gone.

Working feverishly, I poked the two spent shells from the cylinder and slipped two others in place.

I listened, but I heard no sound. Catching hold of the branches of the tree, I pulled myself up, and was surprised that I could do it. The shock that had temporarily put me out of action was wearing off.

My first move was for his rifle, for my own was on the dun, and I had no idea where brother Ralph was. Staggering, I got to the rifle and picked it up, then looked carefully around.

All was quiet again. How many ears had heard those shots and were now listening, I did not know. I only hoped that somewhere out there Penelope was able to listen.

My head still ached, and every step I took was made with caution, for I had no idea how bad a shape I was in. My fingers went to my skull. There was a deep furrow above my ear that had cut the scalp almost to the back of my head. Leading my horse, for even if I could stay in the saddle I would be too easily seen, I started down the gradual slope, which flattened out toward the creek. From time to time I paused, careful to conserve what strength I had.

Before riding away, I studied the area carefully, but there was no sign of life, no movement. What worried me most was that I had no idea what was going on, nor where anybody was. Penelope had been out there in the rocks somewhere, but she had vanished as if she had never been. And across there in the trees Ralph might still be waiting, to say nothing of that poisonous flower, Sylvie.

There were big old cottonwoods and willows along the creek,

and there was water. Once under the trees, I got down and took a long drink. I was hungry, but to risk a fire was to risk my neck. I wasn't that hungry. More than anything else, I wanted to find a place under a safe tree and sleep, but there was no chance of that.

Near me was a huge old cottonwood whose thick leaves rustled and whispered endlessly. Glancing up, I noticed the huge branches and the idea came suddenly.

After tying my horse to a shrub, I rigged a quick sling for my rifle from a couple of piggin strings and then reaching up, I caught the lowest limb of the big tree. Its leaves and the other trees around me offered concealment, and I climbed carefully until I was about twenty feet off the ground and could see all around me.

The first thing I saw was a dust cloud. It was some distance off, downstream, and whoever was causing the dust was out of sight beyond the rocks. My guess made it about half a dozen riders.

Not far away I could see some bones, lying time-whitened under the sun. Were these the bones of Nathan Hume's mule train? I remembered that there had been another battle, a hundred and fifty years before, when an army of Spanish pioneers whipped a huge band of Comanches at this place.

It was very still. The only sound was the gentle rustling of the cottonwood leaves, which never seemed to be quiet. After a few minutes, just as I was about to get down from the tree, I saw Sylvie Karnes come down from the rocks riding a bay pony.

Now where had she gotten that horse? As I watched, she was followed by Steve Hooker, Tex Parker, and two other men whom I did not recognize. This looked to me like too much activity around for one lone Tennessee boy, even if he was a Sackett. My better sense kept telling me I should pull out of here, and fast.

Sylvie by herself was a package of dynamite, and I wanted no part of her. When they discovered Andrew dead—for it was likely they still did not know about it—they would have another reason for hunting me down.

Gold is a hard-won thing, and hard-kept, and when Nathan Hume bought smuggled gold from the Spanish miners in the San Juans he little knew what he was starting. Those old Spanish miners preferred to sell their gold in secret to traders like Hume, rather than have a big part of it taken from them by the Spanish or Mexican governments, to say nothing of the governors of New Mexico. What Hume had started was being played out now, right here.

The group rode out on a little meadow about a quarter of a mile back from the creek and dismounted. They looked as if they were going to camp.

Carefully, I climbed down the tree. My neck was stiff and my head still throbbed with a dull, brow-wrinkling pain, but my muscles seemed to have loosened up. Mounting up, I walked my horse down through the willows and across the creek, which here was only eight to ten inches deep.

The rest of the day I scouted around, searching for the box canyon. All I knew was that it was somewhere north of the Rabbit Ears, which was little enough to go on. And during all that day I stayed clear of the Karnes outfit, riding wide around. Now that they had tied up with Steve Hooker and the boys from Coe's gang, my troubles were multiplied. Of course, I couldn't wish the Coe gang any worse luck than making a deal with Sylvie. She was likely to poison the lot when she got the gold . . . if she got it.

When night came I was far out to the north, and I rode on a few miles and camped on a little creek that emptied into the North Canadian. As I was eight or nine miles from the Rabbit Ears I figured to be pretty safe, so I built myself a fire I could have covered with my hat, and made coffee and broiled myself a steak. I had plenty of fresh meat now, for earlier that day I had killed a yearling buffalo well over to the east.

Just as I was about to pour some coffee, the dun, who was drinking at the creek, suddenly jerked up his head, water dripping from his muzzle, and looked across the creek into the darkness.

Before you could say scat I was back in the darkness with my Winchester cocked and ready.

"Hold easy on that trigger, son, I'm huntin' help, not trouble."

I knew that voice, and while I lay quiet trying to place it in my memory, it spoke again.

"That horse knows me better'n he does you. I gave him to you."

"Come on out then. Show yourself."

"You'll have to give me time. I'm hurt."

Well, I taken a long chance. That voice did sound familiar, and only one man could know how I got that horse. So I went down to the creek and crossed it.

The old man lay in the grass on the far side of the creek, and he was in bad shape. He had been shot more than once, and his left hand was a bloody mess, but he was game. There was no quit in that old man. His kind come from away up the creek, and he was a tough old mossy-horn with a lot of life in him yet.

So I just picked him up and carried him back to camp. He couldn't have weighed more than a hundred and thirty soaking wet, and I'd never seen the day when I couldn't pick up three times that much.

He was in bad shape, but it was his left hand that gave me the turn. Every fingernail was gone, and his fingers all bloody . . . and that could have been no accident.

"Comanches?" I asked.

"In-laws," he said grimly. "Sometimes they can be worse."

"You ain't related to that Karnes outfit?"

"You met up with them?"

"Uh-huh."

First off, I filled a cup with hot, black coffee and held it for him to drink. He was shaky, and he needed something to pick up his spirits a mite. He drank it, taking it in his right hand, while I put on some water to heat up to clean him up with.

"Looks to me as if ever'body on the Staked Plains is related," I said, "and all of them after Nathan Hume's gold."

"I got a claim to it, better than any of the rest."

"Better than Penelope?"

"You don't say. She here?"

"Unless they've killed her, she is. She saved my bacon yesterday, and a fine girl she is."

After he'd drunk the coffee he laid back while I washed out a couple of bullet wounds, neither of them serious, beyond the blood he'd lost. At least, I'd seen men survive worse ones. I always made shift to pack a few wrappings of bandage, for a man on the dodge can't go running to no doctor. So I fixed up the wounds as best I could, and that hand along with it.

The fingernails had been missing for a while, but crawling through the brush he'd evidently torn open the wounds.

"You must have known something they wanted almighty bad."

"I should smile, I did. I knew where that gold was. And I know just where that box canyon is."

"I wonder they let you live."

"They fired my place and then rode off, leaving me hog-tied

in the house. I was out cold and they never figured I'd get out alive. Well, I fooled 'em."

"Seems like everybody in the country started after that gold all to once."

"What would you have me do?" the old man said. "I worked with old Nathan when I was a boy, and I had me a mighty good idea where that gold was, but as long as the widow was alive I didn't figure I had a right to it.

"Others hunted it, but most of them had no idea where to look. I knew how old Nathan thought, and I was sure I could lay hand on the gold. The old man was my cousin, blood-kin, and I was the only one of his flesh who had worked with him. Many a time I went into the San Juans to meet up with the gold traders.

"Them Karneses, they didn't know where I was until you fetched up to their wagon. When they saw that brand on the dun, NH Connected, they knew it for old Nathan Hume's brand, and knew that I was somewhere about. That was one of the reasons they wanted to do away with you."

"Why didn't you try to get the gold before now?"

He glanced up at me. "You ain't seen that place yet, nor heard the stories. Well, I heard 'em. Ain't no Indian alive who will spend a night in that canyon, and mighty few who will even go into it. Evil spirits, they say, and maybe there is."

"You ain't told me your name?"

"Harry Mims. Now don't get me wrong. It wasn't ha'nts kept me out of that box canyon. Mostly it was Comanches. Why, I've lost my outfit twice and nearly lost my hair a couple of times, too.

"One time I was lucky and got right up to the canyon before they come on me. Well, they took my pack outfit and got so busy arguing over the loot that I sneaked off and hid until things quieted down. Took me two weeks to get back to Las Vegas, and when I got there I hadn't enough money for a meal. I got a job swamping in a saloon, then they moved me up to bartender. Took me six months to get myself an outfit again, what with gambling an' all."

"How'd you get clear up here now?"

"A-hossback—how'd you figure? They stole some horses off me, scattered the rest, but those horses come on home, and I caught up a few, saddled up, and rode. I taken me some time, but here I am."

He lay back, resting. He was in such bad shape I didn't feel much like asking him more questions. Somebody had been shooting at him more than a little, and he'd wasted away some, riding all that time. It gave a body the shudders to think what that old man had gone through in getting here.

"What do you figure to do now?"

"You ask a fool question like that? I'm going to get that gold, or stop them from getting it, and by the Lord Harry, I'll kill that Ralph Karnes."

"What about her?"

Harry Mims was still for a while, and then he looked up at me. "Sackett, I know she needs it, but I can't bring myself to kill no woman. Why, she was the worst of all when it came to thinkin' of things to do t' me. It was her thought of the fingernails, and she did part of it herself."

I could believe that of Sylvie.

After a while Mims dropped off to sleep, and I covered him up better. He hadn't told me where his outfit was, but it must be somewhere back in the brush. He couldn't have come far in the shape he was in, not afoot, anyway.

The death of Nathan Hume's widow, way back in Virginia, had opened a fancy show out here on the grasslands of the Panhandle. Everybody and his brother was heading right for the gold, and all at the same time. It was just my luck to land right in the middle of it; and here I was, saddled with an old man who needed help the worst way, and maybe with a girl, if I could find her again.

What about those Indian stories? Now, I was never one to doubt anything an Indian told me. Folks would say they were superstitious and all, but behind most of what they believed there was good common sense. I know one time down Mexico way Indians told me they would never go near a certain place, because there were evil spirits around. Come to find out, there had been a smallpox epidemic there, and that was the Indian way of quarantining the place. They thought evil spirits had caused the smallpox. . . . Well, maybe there was something odd about that box canyon too.

After I'd found Mims's horses—he had four of them . . . two pack animals and a spare saddle horse—I went back to the fire and drank some more coffee, then let the flames die down to the coals. Then when it was fairly dark, I moved my bed back into the darkest shadows, where I could see the old man and the firelit space, and where I'd be unseen by anybody scouting the camp.

Several times during the night I awakened, and each time I lay listening into the night. Finally, near daybreak, I decided not to go back to sleep. Many a night before this I had stayed awake for hours, for in my kind of life a man never knew when he would have to come up shooting.

A long time I lay there thinking of other nights in other places when I had stayed awake listening to the night sounds. It wasn't much of a life, being on the dodge all the time.

After a while I began to hear something. At first it wasn't really a clear sound, only of a sudden my ears seemed to sharpen, for something was moving out there, something that made no sound I could rightly make out.

I looked toward the fire . . . a few red coals still glowed there, and Harry Mims, wrapped in two blankets and a ground sheet, lay dark and silent beside the fire. I could hear his faint breathing.

I reached out with my left hand and took up the edge of the blanket that covered me and put it back carefully. The moccasins I always had with me were close by. Holding my pistol in my right hand, I picked up the moccasins with my left and eased my feet into them.

Picking up a small stone, I tossed it at Mims. It struck his shoulder and his breathing seemed to stop, then it went on again. Was he awake? I had a hunch he was, awake and as ready as a body in his shape could be.

All was quiet, yet with a different sort of quiet now. In the area north of our camp even the night sounds had stopped. Then I heard a faint whisper—the sort of sound a branch can make scraping the side of a man's jeans. Somebody was approaching— perhaps more than one.

I came smoothly and silently to my feet and took a careful step backward, where I was nearer the tree and partly shielded by its branches. Now, even if my bed was seen, I myself was blended into the darkness of the tree.

That gun felt good in my hand, but suddenly I put it back in its holster and drew my knife.

A knife was better for quiet work, in close.

TEN

I waited there in the darkness, knife in hand, thankful its edge was razor-sharp. I held it low, cutting edge up.

Down in the creek there was a rustle of water. Cottonwood leaves whispered softly to the breath of wind. I could smell the wood smoke from the fire, the faint aromatic scent of crushed leaves. Whoever was approaching moved with great skill, for there was not another whisper of sound.

My leg muscles grew tired, but I did not want to shift my feet in a movement that might make even the slightest sound. Anyone who moved as silently as this unknown one would also listen well, for the two are one, to listen and to be conscious of others listening.

Then I saw a shadow where no shadow had been before. I had to look a second time to be sure my eyes were not tricking me into believing something had changed. But the shadow was there. I made a slight move forward, and then my name was breathed. "Mr. Sackett?"

It was Penelope.

My relief was so great that all I could say was, "Where have you been?"

She did not answer, but came swiftly toward me. "Who is that by the fire?"

"Harry Mims. Have you heard of him?"

"I know of him. You'd best awaken him. We must go quickly, before it is light."

"What's happened?"

"Have you ever heard of a man called Tom Fryer? Or Noble Bishop?"

"Are they in this now?"

"Sylvie brought them in. I don't know where she found them, but from all I hear, this only makes things worse."

76

"Is Ferrara with them?"

"There's a slim, dark man. I didn't hear his name. They came into camp tonight, and they seemed to know you."

They knew me all right—it could not have been worse. There were not three more dangerous men west of the Mississippi than those three.

"You are right," I said. "We'd better move."

Mims was sitting up. As we neared the fire he used his good hand to help himself up. "I heard. Let's get out of here. Let's get the gold and run."

It took only a few minutes to roll up our beds and to bring up the horses. Penelope would ride Mims's extra horse, for she didn't have one of her own.

We led our horses to the stream, then mounted and crossed. Mims took the lead, for he was sure he knew where the box canyon lay.

I didn't like the sound of a box canyon, for that meant a trap—a canyon with only one entrance, and the chances were it had steep sides. It smelled like trouble—but then, everything smelled like trouble. I wished again that I had had sense enough to ride out of here before this.

Penelope was close beside me. "You're no tenderfoot," I said. "You couldn't move like that if you were."

"I grew up in the woods in Virginia. I was stalking deer before I was ten."

She'd had no right to make me feel she was helpless, I told myself. It was downright dishonest. Why, she was as good in the woods as I was myself. And she had saved my bacon.

"You pulled me out of trouble." I said it a little grudgingly, for I wasn't used to being bested by a woman. "Thanks."

"That's all right," she said.

"Where's Loomis?" I asked.

"Somewhere around. I lost track of him."

It seemed to me she was neither worried nor sorry. Maybe she already had him figured out. But how about me? How did she know I wouldn't take all that gold and run? I gave her an uneasy look. Could be I was guessing wrong all the way around. But one thing I felt pretty sure of—she wasn't anything like Sylvie Karnes.

When my thoughts turned to Ferrara, Fryer, and Noble Bishop,

I felt a chill. Any one of them was bad enough. All three at once I wanted no part of.

Noble Bishop was a gunman. They told it around that he'd killed twenty men. Cut that by half and it might be true—at least, those killed in known gun battles. Whoever he might have dry-gulched I'd never be knowing, although that sort of thing was more to the taste of Fryer than of Bishop. As for Ferrara, he was a knife man.

All three were known men, hired killers, men for whatever was needed when there was violence to be done. No doubt Sylvie had gotten wind of them through Hooker or one of the others, and she had wasted no time in hiring them.

Harry Mims was old, and he might be crippled now, but he led us as swiftly through the trees as though he could see in the dark. We followed, and when he brought up at the canyon's mouth we came up close to him.

"I don't like it," he said. "The place worries me."

"You're scared?" I was surprised, for that old man was tough. At any other time he might have gone for his gun at the very question.

"Call it what you like. Maybe the Indians know what they're talking about. I don't like that canyon, and never did."

"You've been here before?"

"Yes. . . . It's a litter of bones in there. More than one man has died in that place."

"Sure. Nathan Hume's pack train died there, or most of them. Their bones will be there—what else would you expect?"

"There's others," he said soberly. "I tell you, I don't like the place."

"Let's get the gold then, and get out. If we don't do that, we might as well leave right now, because they'll be coming and I'm not one to fight without cause."

The dun didn't like the canyon either. He tried to turn away, fought the bit, and did all he could to avoid entering. The other horses were nervous, but none of them behaved as badly as the dun.

We rode in, darkness closed around us. Up ahead of us, Harry Mims coughed, and then drew up. "Like it or not, we'll have to wait until daylight. There's a pool covered with green scum, and there's some holes around here too. God knows what's in them, but I'd not like to be."

We sat our horses then, no one of us wanting to get down from the saddle, though no one of us could have said why. It was simply an uneasy feeling we had, and the way the horses acted. I know I had no wish to trust the dun with me out of the saddle, unless he was strongly tied.

Presently a saddle creaked. "I'm getting down," Penelope said. "I'm going to look around."

"Wait!" I spoke sharply. "This may be a damned trap. Get back in your saddle and wait."

Well, I expected a quick answer, but none came. She got back into the saddle and sat quietly. By now the sky was growing gray, and it would not be very long until it was light enough to see.

Nobody said anything for several minutes, and then it was Mims who spoke. "Say I'm scared if you like, but I can't get shut of this place fast enough."

Rocks and brush began to take shape, and we could see the walls of the canyon. Nobody was going to ride out of here unless he went out the front way. Or so I thought then.

"I could do with a cup of coffee," I said.

"Not there. Let's get the gold and get out."

"It won't be that easy," I said. "It never is."

Nevertheless, I was as eager to be away as he was, for the canyon was a depressing place. Bones lay about, and not all of them seemed old enough to be the remains of Nathan Hume's pack train.

We all saw the pool, which lay close to Penelope's horse. A still, dead place covered with a scum of green. Penelope leaned over and stirred the surface with a branch she broke from a dead tree. The water under the scum was oily and dark.

"You notice something?" Harry Mims said suddenly. "There ain't no birds in here. I've seen no insects, either. Maybe them Indians are right."

The place was beginning to give me the creeps. "All right," I said. "From what I've heard the gold should be somewhere yonder."

We worked our way around the fallen rocks and over to the spot. There were bones enough, all right. A mule's jaw, white and ancient, lay near a shattered rib cage. But the skeletons weren't

pulled apart, the way they often are after wolves or coyotes have
worried at them.

I could see that the canyon walls were too steep for any horse
to climb, in some places too steep for a man. Yet the first sign of
life I saw in the canyon were the tracks of wild horses. Several
horses had come through here not long since, but there were older
tracks, too, which were headed toward the back of the canyon. On
a hunch, I swung my horse around. "You hunt the gold," I said.
"There's something back there I've got to see."

Without waiting for a reply, I started off on the trail of those
mustangs, and believe me, the dun was ready to move. He just
didn't take to that box canyon, not at all.

Those wild horses headed right back up the canyon and into
a mess of boulders tumbled from the rock wall above. They wound
around among the rocks and brush, and of a sudden I found myself
on a narrow trail going up a steep crack in the rocks, scarcely wide
enough for a man on horseback. It went straight up, then took a
turn, but I had no doubt but that it topped out on the mesa above.

So there was another way out.

Suddenly I heard a faint call, and turned in the saddle to look
back. I hadn't realized I had come so far, or so much higher. I
could see Penelope back there, a tiny figure waving her arm at
me.

When I reached them Mims was down on the ground. He
was lying on his face, which I saw had a faint bluish tinge when I
turned him over. "Let's get him out of here," I said quickly. "If
they come on us with him out—"

I'd no idea what was wrong with him, but it looked as if he'd
fainted from some cause or other, and his heart seemed a mite
rapid, but was beating all right. I got him up in the saddle and
lashed him there, then led the way down the canyon and out. We
rode at once toward the shelter of the trees but saw no one, and
soon were back among the cottonwoods and willows along the
creek.

By that time the better air outside the canyon, and maybe the
movement on the back of his horse, seemed to have done him
some good. I took him down from the saddle, feeling uncommonly
helpless, not knowing what to do for him; but after a moment or
two he began to come around.

"You given to passing out?" I asked. "What happened back there?"

"I don't know. All of a sudden I felt myself going. I tell you one thing—I want no more of that box canyon. There's something wrong about that place. Call it whatever you like, I think that place is ha'nted."

After a while he sat up, but his face was uncommonly pale. When he tried to drink he couldn't keep it down.

"Whatever we do had best be done quickly," I said. "There are too many others around. They'll find the place if we waste time."

"Maybe I'd best go after the gold. I can take along one of the horses and pack some of it out, and I can get the rest on my horse."

Penelope stood there looking at me, and then she said, "Mr. Sackett, you must think I am a very foolish girl, to let you go after that gold alone."

"No, ma'am. You feel up to it, you just go along by yourself— maybe you'd feel safer that way. But I figure one of us ought to stay by Mr. Mims here."

"I can get along," said Mims. "You can both go."

To tell the truth, I'd no great urge to go back there at all, and even less so if I went along with Penelope. She had helped me out of a fix, but she needed my help. I didn't figure it would be easy to get that gold out, and I wanted nothing else to worry about—especially not a girl I had to look after. I said as much.

"You look after yourself," she told me, speaking sharp but not what you'd call angry. And with that she got into the saddle and I followed.

To see us, you wouldn't figure we were going after a treasure like three hundred pounds of gold. We didn't act very willing, and the closer we came to the mouth of that canyon the slower we rode. I didn't like it, and neither did she.

Harry Mims was a tough old man, but something had put him down, and it was nothing we could see. Maybe there was a peculiar smell, time to time. I never mentioned it, not really knowing whether it was imagination, or something more.

It was almost at the mouth of the canyon that we rode right into a trap.

Penelope might have had an excuse, but there wasn't anything like that for me—I should have known better. All of a sudden, there was Sylvie, standing right out in front of us, and when we both drew up, men started stepping out from the rocks and brush.

They had us, all right. They had us cold. And a prettier lot of thieves you never did see. Bishop was there, and Ralph Karnes. Hooker was there, too, his arm in a sling. And there was Charlie Hurst and Tex Parker and Bishop's men.

"Well, Mr. Sackett," Sylvie said, "it looks as if we can pick up the chips."

"Don't figure on it."

She just smiled at me, but when she looked at Penelope she was not smiling. "And now I've got you," she said, and there was an ugly ring to her voice. "Right where I've wanted you."

"Where's that canyon?" Bishop asked.

It sounded like an odd question, for from where he sat he could almost have thrown a rock into the mouth of it, but the way it looked we were about to ride right past it. The reason was that you had to ride to the far side before you could get past the big boulders at the mouth.

"Canyons all around, Noble. You take your pick." I gestured right toward the canyon. "Like that one, for instance."

He grinned at me. "You already checked that one," he said. "We found your tracks coming out. If you left that canyon the gold can't be there. So you show us."

"I wish we knew. How's a man going to pick one canyon out of all these around here?"

"You'd better find a way," Bishop said.

"Don't be a damn fool, Noble. Look, we've been up here a few days now. How long does it take to pick up that much gold and run? If we knew where it was, we'd have been off and running. Nathan Hume was supposed to have hidden some gold up here. We know that two men got away from the massacre. Maybe some others did, too."

"Two?" Sylvie spoke up. She hadn't known that.

"Sure, there was a Mexican got away—he was a packer for Hume. But the governor of New Mexico was after anybody who worked for him. Somebody tipped off the governor that Hume was smuggling gold out and paying no percentage to the government, or whatever they had to do in those days.

"That Mexican lit out for Mexico, but he got his back broke

down there and never could come back. But that doesn't say some
of his folks mightn't have come back."

"Are you trying to tell us the gold isn't there?" Ralph demanded incredulously.

"I'd say it isn't," I replied. "Bishop, I don't know about you,
but Fryer worked the mining camps in Nevada and Colorado. He'll
tell you hidden gold is usually gone, or nobody ever finds it. There's
men who have spent their lives hunting for treasure like this, and
never found anything."

"That's nonsense," Ralph said. "The gold is here...we know
it is."

"Lot's of luck. I only hired on to guide these folks into this
country. You find it, you can have it. And you'll know the place
by the bones."

"Bones?" It was the first time Ferrara had spoken.

"Sure. A lot of men died there when Hume was killed, and a
lot have died since. The Comanches and the Utes say that box
canyon is cursed. No Indian will spend a night in the canyon, and
none will ride through if they can help it."

"See?" Hooker said. "That was what I was tellin' you."

"Take their weapons," Sylvie said. "We will make them talk."

"Noble," I said, "nobody ain't about to take my guns. Do you
think I'd shuck my iron, with what I know's ahead? I've got nothing
to tell you, so there'd be no end to it. You boys want what I'm
holdin', you're going to have to buy it the hard way."

"Don't talk like a fool!" Ralph said. "Why, we could blow you
out of your saddle!"

"Likely. Only Noble here knows me, and he knows I wouldn't
be goin' alone. I seen a man one time who was still shooting with
sixteen bullets in him. At this range I know I'm going to get two
of you anyway—maybe three or four."

And they were going to help me do it, for if trouble started I
was going to jump my horse right in the middle of them, where
every shot they fired would endanger everybody else in their party.

Now, Noble Bishop was no damn fool. He'd used a gun enough
to know that you don't just shoot somebody and they fall down. If
a man is mad and coming at you, you have to get him right through
the heart, right through the brain, or on a big bone to stop him.
On the other hand, a shot that's unexpected can drop a man in his

tracks; although any expert on gun-shot wounds can tell some strange stories about what can happen in a shooting.

Bishop knew I'd been wild and desperate. He knew I was reckoned to be a fast man with a gun, and a dead shot; and he knew if it came to shooting, somebody was going to get killed. In such a melee it could be anybody. And like I'd hinted, the gold might not even be there.

Bishop, Fryer, Ferrara, and maybe Parker were canny enough to guess what I'd do, and they weren't having any of it. After all, why start a gunfight when they could pick us off one at a time with small risk? Or let us find the gold and then take it from us? I knew how they were thinking, because I knew what I'd think in their place.

Bishop spoke calmly. "He's right as rain." He wasn't going to turn this into a wild shooting where anybody could get hurt, and maybe nothing accomplished in the end.

Time and numbers were on their side. All the help I had was a girl and a crippled-up old man, but both of them could scatter a lot of promiscuous lead at such close-up range as this.

"There's nothing to be gained by shooting it out here," Bishop went on. "You ride on your business and we'll ride on ours."

Sylvie was about to protest, then said. "Let him go. Just kill the girl. She has claim to that gold." You never did see anybody who looked so beautiful and was so poison mean as she did when she said it.

"Nobody gets shot," Bishop said. "You all turn and ride out of here."

We turned and started away, but as I went past Bishop, I said to him in a low voice, "Noble, if you find that gold, don't drink any coffee she makes."

Then we went on by, but when I glanced back he was still watching us. After a minute, he lifted a hand and waved. That was all.

"I thought surely there would be shooting," Penelope said.

"Nobody'd been drinking," Mims said dryly, "and nobody was crazy. We'd have wound up with some of them shot up, and nothing settled."

All the same, nothing was settled anyway. Noble Bishop and me would have it to do, come the right day.

And I had an idea the day was not far off.

ELEVEN

Sylvie Karnes must have made contact with Bishop in Romero, I was thinking. But murderous as Bishop was, he did his work with a gun, which in my book was something altogether different from using poison. Yet he was none the less deadly, for all of that.

"How'd you get shut of Loomis?" I asked as we rode along.

Penelope shrugged. "Who said I was? We got separated, that's all."

Now, I didn't really believe that, nor did I believe that I'd seen the last of that stiff-necked, hard-mouthed old man.

"Whatever we're going to do," I added, "had best be done soon." Even as I said it, I had no stomach for it. I'd a sight rather face Bishop with a gun than ride back into that box canyon.

And Mims was in bad shape. He had lost blood, leaving him weak as a cat, and he could only fumble with his bad hands. It was no wonder he had passed out up there in the canyon, but the idea stayed with me that it had been something worse than mere weakness.

The shadows were growing long as we rode along the stream and then crossed to a low island covered with willows. It was no more than sixty or seventy feet long and half as wide, but there was concealment of a sort there, and some grass.

Swinging down, I helped Mims from the saddle, and felt him trembling with weakness. I spread his blankets, and got him over to them, and he let himself down with a deep sigh.

"We'd better make some coffee," Penelope said. "We all need it."

The stars were out while I gathered driftwood along the island's low shore, and the water rustled pleasantly. Behind the trunk of a huge old cottonwood deadfall, I put together a small fire. The

85

wind was picking up a little, and it worried me, for the sound of the wind would cover anybody trying to approach us.

Nobody talked. All of us were tired, and on edge. We all needed rest, Mims most of all. When I looked at the old man it gave me a twist of pain inside. And it gave me a sudden turn to think that though I was young and strong and tough now, this was the way a man could be when he grew old. It was old age I could see in the face of Harry Mims now.

He drank some coffee, but refused anything to eat, and soon he fell into a restless sleep. Off to one side I said to Penelope, "All the gold in this country ain't worth that man's life. He's a good old man."

"I know." Then she was silent. I sipped black coffee and tried to reach out with my thoughts and picture what tomorrow would bring.

"I need that money, Nolan," she went on. "I need it badly. Say I am selfish if you will, but if I don't get the gold, I'll have nothing, nothing at all."

There didn't seem much of anything to say to that, and I kept still. But I kept thinking about the gold.

We were not far from the canyon. As I thought about it, I wondered if I could find my way around in there in the dark. The trouble was they would probably have somebody watching. Tired as I was, I wanted to get it over with and get out of there.

That canyon worried me. A man who lives on the rough side of things learns to trust to his instincts. The life he leads calls for a kind of alertness no man living a safe and regular life would need; his senses become sharper and they make him alive to things he can't always put into words. I was not a superstitious man, but there was something about that canyon that was all wrong.

After a bit of contemplating, I decided not to go there by night. It would be hard enough to come upon the gold in the daylight, let alone prowling among boulders and rock slides in the dark, and maybe falling into a hole, nobody knew how deep.

Most of all I wanted to get shut of Loomis and Sylvie and Ralph, and I got to thinking about what kind of people they were. With western folks a body knew where he stood. I mean, things were mostly out in the open, for the very good reason that there was no place to hide anything. People were scarce, the towns were small, and whatever a man did it had to be pretty well known.

Things were beginning to change, though, because with the railroads a new kind of folks were coming west. The cheats and the weaklings that hard times had weeded out in the earlier years could now ride west on the cushions.

Jacob Loomis was a man who might have come at any time, though he wouldn't have been any great addition to the country. Sylvie and Ralph would not have come west at all but for the gold they thought they'd come by in an easy way.

Bishop might try to shoot me, I knew. Fryer might try dry-gulching me, but that was to be expected, more or less; anyway, this was Indian country where a man had to be on guard. Poison was another matter, and Sylvie and Ralph . . . well, there was something wrong about them, something evil, something twisted in their minds.

Finally I went to sleep, though I knew when I closed my eyes that I would wake up to a day of guns and gunsmoke. There would be blood on the rocks of the Rabbit Ears before another sundown.

The last stars hung lonely in the sky, and a low wind trembled the cottonwood leaves when my eyes opened and my ears reached out for sound. One by one I heard the sounds—the rustling leaves, the low murmur of the creek water, the pleasant sound of horses cropping grass. Out in the creek a fish jumped.

Picking up my boots, I shook them out—centipedes or scorpions have a way of crawling into boots at night; and then I tugged them on, stood up, and stamped them into place. My hat was already on, of course. First thing any cowhand does of a morning is put on his hat. I slung my gun belt and settled the holster into place, then tied the thong about my leg.

It was not yet full daylight. A single red coal showed in the fire. I stretched the stiffness out of me, wiped the night sweat from my Winchester, and went down to the creek to wash and to brush my teeth with a frayed willow stick.

Moving quietly, I went to the dun and rubbed his ears a mite, talking to him in a low, friendly tone. Then I saddled up, rolled my bed, and made ready to move out.

The old man was sleeping, breathing evenly. That tough old man, all bone and rawhide, would pull through all right. As for that girl Penelope—

She was gone. Her bed was there, but she had slipped away. Her horse was gone too.

My mustang hadn't made any fuss because she came from within the camp, she was one of us, and she had a right to go. And for once I'd slept so sound I'd missed her going.

She had no business slipping off that way, but I had no business sleeping so sound that she could do it. The truth was, it made me mad to think anybody could slip out of camp without me knowing— but it worried me, too. My life depended on never sleeping that sound.

Kneeling down, I touched Mims on the shoulder. He opened his eyes right off, sharp and clear as if he had never slept.

"That girl kin of yours slipped off. No telling what's happened to her."

He sat up and reached for his hat. "She'll have gone to that misbegotten canyon. We'd better get over there."

Whilst he got himself up, I slapped a saddle on his horse, and only minutes after he opened his eyes we had all gear packed and ready, and rode out of camp.

We walked our horses out of the creek and started up through the trees. The Rabbit Ears bulked large and dark against the sky. A quail called somewhere out in the brush. I knew we were riding to a showdown, and for once I wished it was over.

We kept to low ground, seeking all the cover we could find, and riding out in the open only when we reached the canyon mouth. There seemed to be plenty of tracks, but we could make nothing of them. As before, the dun wanted no part of the box canyon, but at my urging he went ahead hesitantly. I could see that several horses had entered the canyon since we had come out of it.

The first thing we saw was Steve Hooker, and he was dead. He lay crumpled on the ground, one knee drawn up, his six-gun still in its holster, the thong in place.

"Look!" Mims said hoarsely. He was pointing at Hooker's tracks.

He had been walking along, taking slightly shorter strides than a man of his height might have been expected to take, which made me sure he had come in here after dark. Walking on uneven ground, unfamiliar to him, a man will usually take shorter steps.

He had fallen after a few staggering steps and had gone to his hands and his knees. He had gotten up and gone on, and then had fallen again. This time when he had risen he took not more than two or three steps before he collapsed.

"Something last night," Mims spoke in a low, awed tone. "Sack-ett, I'm riding the hell out of here."

"You wait just a minute," I said. "No use goin' off half-cocked."

Nothing seemed any different from yesterday except for the body of Hooker. I stepped down from the saddle and turned him over. There was no sign of a wound, no blood. His face looked puffy and had a kind of bluish color to it, but that might have been the effect of the early light, or it might have been my imagination.

The low clouds that had come with daybreak hung over the Rabbit Ears, and tails of mist drifted past them. The canyon was a gloomy place at any time with its dark, basaltic rock and the uncanny stillness. I heard no sound at all, and saw no birds, no small animals.

What was it the Mexican had told me that night on the Neuces?

The gold had been pushed into a hole under a boulder, and rocks had been caved in over it. A cross had been scratched on the rock. Forty years or more had passed since the day that hap-pened—I didn't have a sure idea when it was that Nathan Hume had been caught in this trap and massacred.

"Look for a white cross, Mims," I said, keeping my voice low, not knowing who there might be listening. "The sort of thing a man would scratch on a rock if he was in a hurry."

We both saw it at the same moment and started our horses toward it.

The gray clouds seemed darker and lower still, and there was a hint of dampness in the air. I did not like the feel of it; I did not like anything about this strange, haunted place.

Dropping my Winchester into the boot, I swung down from the saddle, and tied the dun to some stiff brush nearby. I loosened the thong from my six-shooter, then walked into the hollow where the boulder stood. At the base of it, below the scratched cross, was a jumble of tumbled rock.

I looked all around. "Keep a sharp lookout, Mims," I said. "Don't watch me—watch for them."

"I wonder where that girl is?" Mims said in a worried tone. "She'd no call to go traipsing off like that."

"Let's get the gold. Then we'll hunt for her. I've got a hunch she can take care of herself."

The hiding place was logical enough. Men defending themselves from Indians would probably retreat to just such a place as this. It would have seemed a good place to make a stand, although Indians up on the rim could have covered them with rifle fire.

One by one I started moving the rocks, most of them slabs, or boulders from head-size on up. I worked as fast as a body could, but I was trying to make as little noise as possible. It was not so much that I suspected anybody was close by, but there was something about that canyon that made a man want to walk softly and speak in a low tone.

My head, which had only stopped aching the day before, started in again now, and my breathing was bad. After a bit I left the hollow and scrambled up beside my horse, to lean against him. It was a surprising thing to know how much a wallop on the head could take out of a man.

Mims looked worried. "You feel all right? You sure don't look so good."

"Headache," I told him, "from that knock on the head from Andrew's bullet."

He looked at me thoughtfully. "Now, you never did tell me how come your head was like that. Andrew, hey? What become of him?"

"Come to think of it, it wasn't Andrew who shot me, it was Ralph. It was Andrew who came in to finish the job."

The air was better up there beside my horse—only a few feet difference, too. After a few minutes I slid back down and went to work again, but I had moved only a few boulders when my head began to buzz and I felt very peculiar. I was going to have to quit.

"If there was a swamp around here," Mims said, "I'd figure you were getting a dose of marsh gas. It'll sometimes do that to a man. Cuts his wind."

Crawling up again, I staggered to my horse, took my canteen and rinsed my mouth with water, and then emptied some of the water over my head. After a moment or two I felt better and went down into the hollow once more. Almost at once I found the gold.

It had been dumped into a natural hollow in the rock underneath. Wasting no time, I began to get it out.

Mims, despite his weakness, got down and started to help. Our excitement carried us on, with me passing the ingots up to Mims, who put them in the prepared packs on his two lead horses.

There was no question of silence any more. I was coughing

and choking, and couldn't seem to stop. But I knew that at any moment the others might come.

When the last of the gold was loaded, I climbed up to where the horses stood, not more than six or eight feet above where the gold had been hidden. I fell down, pulled myself up, and then untying my horse, I got a leg over the saddle.

The dun wasted no time, but started for the steep trail up the mountain. It was that which saved us.

I was coughing so hard I could scarcely do more than stay in the saddle. Harry Mims was right behind me with the gold. We had started up the trail when far back behind us we heard a clatter of hoofs and saw several riders come into the canyon. The first thing they saw was Hooker, and then the marks of our horses' hoofs where they had waited while we loaded the gold. They saw the hollow among the rocks, where I'd climbed down to get at the gold, and they saw the empty hole. While they were flocked around it our horses were still scrambling up the steep trail.

We were still within rifle range when they saw us. The gold had been there... and now they were seeing it slip away from them.

Which one of them fired the shot, I will never know, nor how many of them there were. I know Tex Parker was there, or somebody riding his horse, and a man wearing a Mexican sombrero, who might have been Charlie Hurst. There was no sign of Bishop, nor of Penelope. All that I saw at that one quick glance, for I never got another.

One man whipped his rifle to his shoulder and fired, I saw the leap of flame from the muzzle, and then the whole world seemed to blow up in our faces. There was a tremendous explosion and an enormous flame shot up out of the canyon.

I hit the ground with a jarring thud, and I never knew whether I was blown from my saddle or thrown by my startled horse. Only I lit on my hands and knees, looking down into the canyon but well back from the edge.

Flame was streaking out in rushing streams from the point of the explosion, seeming to seek out every hollow, every low place among the rocks, and then it hit a three-foot-wide hole in the rocks. We'd seen that hole, but we hadn't gone near it.

Now the mouth of the hole was a great jet of flame, and the air was filled with a terrible, continuing roar.

Pulling myself to my feet, I staggered away, filled with horror, and trying to get away from the sound of the roaring.

There was no sign of my horse, and none of Harry Mims or the pack horses, but for several minutes the only thing I could think of was that I wanted to get away.

I climbed up, and had gone almost half a mile before I saw Mims. He was still in the saddle, and he had the pack horses with him. He was trying to round up the line-back dun, but the mustang was frightened and would have none of him.

Slowly, I limped along the mountainside toward them. The dun shied several times, but finally he stood still and let me get into the saddle.

We rode straight away toward the west, with no thought in our minds but to get away from that dreadful sight and that terrible sound. I'd seen men die before, but never like that.

And where... *where was Penelope?*

TWELVE

Neither of us felt like talking. We rode straight ahead, but we had no destination in mind. It was simply that we wanted to get away from the box canyon, away from that awful scene.

It was Mims who finally spoke. "Must be some kind of gas... or oil. You hear about that feller back in Pennsylvania who drilled him an oil well? Supposing something like that caught fire?"

I didn't know the answer, but it seemed as if it must have been something of the sort. Even the fact that we had the gold, three hundred pounds of it, was forgotten in the shock of what had happened in the canyon.

What brought me back to myself was the thought of Penelope.... Where was she? Loomis, I was sure, had not been among these in the canyon. There had been at least four or five men down there, and Fryer and Ferrara might have been among them, or perhaps some other friends of Parker and Hurst.

"We've got to get under cover," I said, "and we've got to stash this gold somewhere."

I was still coughing from whatever it was I'd gotten into my lungs down there—the same thing probably that had killed Steve Hooker. It might have been worse for him at nighttime, or maybe his heart was bad. We'd never know about that, and I wasn't giving it much thought. It was the living I was concerned with.

Steve Hooker had charted his own course, followed his own trail. If it led him to the death he'd found, he had probably saved himself from a bullet or a noose, for he was headed for one or the other. When a man begins a life of violence, or when he decides to live by taking something away from others, he just naturally points himself toward one end. He can't win—the odds are too much against him.

We kept heading west, riding at a steady gait for about four miles, and then I let Mims go on ahead with the pack horses while I did what I could to wipe out whatever trail we had left through the bunch grass.

When I came up to him again, walking my horse up Cienequilla Creek, he had stopped at a place barren of cover—a sandy bank rising a few feet above the shore of the creek. It was just what we wanted. We unloaded the gold and put it down close to the bank, then caved the bank over it. The sand was dry, and when we had finished there was no sign that this spot was any different from any other place along the banks where small slides or cave-ins were common. Wiping out our own tracks, we started back.

It was early—the sun wasn't more than an hour above the horizon. The sky was darkened by the pall of smoke above Rabbit Ears, but the smoke seemed to be thinning out some, we thought.

We had to find Penelope, if she was alive, and I was surely thinking she was. She just had to be.

Slipping off in the middle of the night like that . . . it made no kind of sense unless she figured to get to the gold before we did, or anybody else.

But what happened to her? She had not been in the canyon, of that I was sure, so something must have stopped her, or turned her aside.

Presently I said to Mims, "I never figured to see you again after you loaning me that horse. Main thing I wanted then was distance."

"They had a rope for you, all right, and I never did see such an outfit." Mims chuckled. "Mad? They were really scratching dirt and butting heads. Fact is, they talked some about lynching me on general principles."

"What stopped 'em?"

"I had me an old ten-gauge shotgun in the cabin. After you taken off I just went back and loaded her up. Time or two I've noticed that a ten-gauge shotgun is quite a pacifier. Folks who get riled up and want to twist somebody's tail sort of calm down when they see one.

"Well, they rode up, just a stompin' and a-chawin', so I showed 'em the shotgun and told 'em you wanted a horse in a hurry and I let you have one.

"I just wished I'd of had that shotgun ready when Sylvie showed up. I never did shoot no woman, but there's one I figure I could shoot with a clear conscience."

By now we had picked up Rabbit Ears Creek and were working our way around to the south side of the mountain, all the while scouting for tracks. And soon we found them.

They were buckboard tracks, leading north past the east side of the mountain. We slowed our pace and followed, riding with rifles ready for trouble.

We found a camp that had been used for a couple of days, but was deserted now. We could be only a few miles from the box canyon, and their next camp must be close by. We were getting smoke from the fire in the canyon now; it was thin, but there was a-plenty of it.

Harry Mims drew up. "Nolan, I ain't much on the scare, but we're sure askin' for trouble. That outfit's got to be close by, and they'll be in a sweat to get that gold or our hides."

"That girl needs help," I said, "and I can't ride off without seeing her safe. It ain't in me."

"What kinda outlaw are you?"

"I ain't figured that out yet, but I surely ain't riding away until she's safe."

We had started on again, keeping under cover of brush and trees, and pulling up every now and again to listen.

Suddenly we came upon the buckboard—or what was left of it. It had been pushed off a little bank, brush thrown over it, and then set afire. There was little left but the wheel rims, the hubs, and some charred spokes. A smell of smoke still hung over it.

Neither of us could make much out of the tracks except that somebody had charged off the side of the hill and stampeded the buckboard horses. There had been a fight, for we found some empty shells, a bullet scar on a tree, and the earth churned up by the hoofs of several horses.

"I'll bet they didn't get Flinch," Mims commented. "From what you tell of that breed, he'd be a sly one."

It was mid-afternoon now. We listened but there wasn't a sound.

We rode on under a low sky made darker by the oily smoke still coming from the fire in the canyon. We held to the bottoms, alert for trouble. How Mims felt I could guess, and I knew that I was all in. Seemed like we'd been running and riding forever.

What I wanted now was some sitting-around time and eating three square meals a day. I wanted coffee I didn't make myself, and some restaurant-cooked grub.

We had come up the east side of the Rabbit Ears and had reached the creek again. Now we smelled woodsmoke, and we took our horses down to the damp sand along the edge of the creek.

There was a peck of trouble standing out for us somewhere close ahead, and we both knew it. You just don't ride up to a crowd like that without expecting trouble. And there'd be one woman there, maybe two. The women worried me most of all. You might figure out what a man would do, but never a woman.

An old outlaw told me one time, "Look out for the women. You never know whether they're going to scream, or faint, or go for a gun."

And they were there, all right, both of them. When we rode up the two of them were facing each other alongside the fire.

Jacob Loomis was sitting on a rock facing toward us, his blanket roll beside him. Noble Bishop was there, his face still, eyes watchful, missing nothing. And Fryer... I'd sort of figured him for one of those who died back in the canyon, but here he was, big as life and twice as ugly. And the Mexican was beside him.

Flinch worried me most of all. He wasn't there.

Loomis' eyes took on an ugly shine when we rode up through the trees. Bishop looked at me, but he made no move of any kind. With Bishop and me it was a cut-and-dried thing. Each of us had a reputation as a fast man with a gun, and each of us knew that if it came to shooting somebody was going to get hurt. Neither was eager to try the other, but each of us knew that events might push us that way.

What was going on when we rode up I didn't wait to find out, but I knew it was something that had to be stopped.

"Penelope," I said, "it's all over now. We'll ride with you to Santa Fe."

Bishop turned his eyes to me. "What happened over there?"

"That canyon must have been full of gas from oil underground. It seeped out and, being heavy like, it held close to the ground in the low places. Me an' Harry here, we were up on the rim, and one of them—I don't know who—got skittish and fired a shot.

"You know how this black powder is. A flame jumped from

the muzzle when he shot, and the whole canyon blew up all to once, with streamers of fire wherever gas had gathered. Those men never had them a chance."

"We rode over that way," Bishop said. "We couldn't make out much, and we didn't stay long. All we could see was rocks blackened by fire and that hole in the rocks shooting out a jet of fire."

"How long do you reckon it will burn?" Fryer asked.

"Who knows? Years, maybe. It'll burn as long as there's anything left to burn."

"What about the gold?" Ralph Karnes demanded.

I shrugged. "What about it? Looks to me like nobody's going to get at that gold for a good long time."

"Unless," Sylvie said, looking right at me, "somebody got it out before the fire started."

"There's always that," I admitted. "But it looked to me like all those fellows got to it at once. I don't think any of them got out alive."

"I wasn't thinking of them," Sylvie said. "I was thinking of you."

Nobody said anything for a minute, but Penelope was looking at me, her eyes bright with the questions in them. I was hoping they would wait.

"Well," I said, smiling easier than I felt like, "if I had that gold I'd be splittin' the breeze for Denver right now. I surely wouldn't be wastin' time talking to you folks."

"Neither would I," Fryer said. "What would he come back for?"

"For her," Sylvie said. "Can't you see he's got an itch for Penelope?"

They were all looking at me, and I just shrugged. I wasn't looking at Pen when I spoke. "You're funnin' me, Sylvie. With all that money no man's going to have to look for women; he'll just have to look out for them. Why, if a man rides into Denver with all that gold he'll be combin' them out of his hair.

"Now, Penelope here is a nice girl. We promised to see her safe into Santa Fe. Mims here is a relative of hers."

I knew about where we stood. Fryer believed me easy enough, and so did the Mexican. Bishop . . . well, he was holdin' court in his mind—he hadn't come to any decision yet. Sylvie and Loomis, they were so crooked they wouldn't believe anybody and they were suspicious of everybody. Sylvie, I knew, would never let us ride out of there if she could figure some way to do us in. And I knew that, money or not, Jake Loomis wanted Penelope. He wanted her right out in these hills with nobody around. I could see the purpose in him, and the cruelty.

Right then, I guess, I made up my mind it was going to be a shooting matter.

The last thing I wanted was to swap lead with Bishop in that crowd. Likely he felt the same way, but Sylvie or Ralph or maybe Loomis would surely trigger trouble unless we could get out of here quick.

"Mount up, Pen," I said, "we're riding out."

Even as I spoke my mind was laying out the whole scene, taking everything in.

The bank of the creek was low and flat, just rising a mite near the edge of the trees that surrounded the clearing. There were a few good-sized boulders close by. Some of their horses were back on the left, standing under the trees. Penelope's horse, loaned her by Mims, was over with the team from the buckboard. The harness had been stripped off and both of them now wore Indian-style bridles, made by Flinch, I'd bet.

"She's not going," Sylvie said. "This is family trouble, and we'll settle it here."

Bishop wasn't talking. I wanted to know where he stood, but as long as I didn't make a point of it he could wait and listen.

"There's no reason for trouble," I said, "family or no family. You and Ralph go your own way and she can go hers."

"We found Andrew," Ralph said.

Well, here it was. The whole thing was shaping up now just the way I thought it would, but had hoped it wouldn't.

"You shot me, Ralph," I said, "and Andrew figured to finish the job. He didn't quite make it."

"I think you've got the gold," Loomis said. "Why else would you be so ready to ride off?"

I shrugged. "Why waste time around here? The show's over."

Sylvie suddenly seemed to give in. "All right. Let's forgive and forget. We were just getting ready for supper. Get down and I'll pour some coffee."

This has gone on long enough. "I don't like your coffee, Sylvie. It comes out a mite strong for my taste. Pen, you get your horse. We're leaving . . . now."

Pen started toward the horses and Sylvie sprang at her. All I needed was to move in to help her and somebody would take a shot at me.

But Pen didn't need any help. Sylvie tried to grab at her hair with both hands, but Pen wasn't having any. She let her have it.

Well, I couldn't believe it. Seemed I'd never learn. Here was that girl I was always for protecting, and she needed no more protection than a mountain lion. Sylvie sprang at her, hands up-raised, and Pen hit her right in the stomach with a doubled-up fist. When Sylvie gasped for breath and brought her hands down, Pen slapped her across the mouth with a crack like a pistol shot. Then she caught up the reins of her horse and swung up.

"Stop her!" Loomis shouted. "Bishop, you stop her—or give me a gun and I will!"

Bishop never moved. He just glanced over at Loomis and said, "You better be happy, old man, that you ain't got a gun. Nolan Sackett would kill you."

So we rode out of there and started west again. But I was worried. Noble Bishop would be wanting that gold, and how much of my story he believed I didn't know. Only thing I was sure of was that he hadn't wanted a shoot-out down there by the creek. There were too many people and too many guns, and it would be a matter of luck, not skill, if a man survived. There were too many chances of a wild bullet doing what you didn't mean an aimed bullet to do.

We rode fast. We were going to pick up that gold and ride out of there, and I was hoping I'd seen the last of all of them.

We were northeast of the Rabbit Ears now, and the peaks were red with the dying sun. There was a dull glow over the canyon and we could hear, even at this distance, the roar.

We headed for Rabbit Ears Creek, and from time to time I turned in my saddle, but nobody was following us that I could see. By the time we were due south of the mountain the stars were coming out and it was well on toward dark.

"They won't leave it alone, Sackett," Mims said. "They'll come."

"Sure, they will."

Penelope had not done any talking, and I was just as pleased. I was still mad over her riding out and leaving us in the night that way.

Taking the bulk of Cienequilla del Barro Mountain for a land-mark, I kept on west and when it was well after dark I changed direction several times until we were close under the shadow of the mountain. Then we switched and turned northeast toward the creek where the gold had been buried.

Mims drew up suddenly. "Sackett, I don't like the smell of this. Something's wrong."

Of course it was . . . but what? It had gone off too easy, altogether too easy. I was sure we had not been followed, but what if there had been no need? Supposing we had been observed earlier in the day? Observed in the vicinity, even if not while burying the gold.

Maybe they knew approximately where we had gone, but not exactly. There was a good deal of smoke, the clouds were low, and there might have been intervening trees or brush. As I thought of it, it was plain enough to me that they might have been watching from up on the Rabbit Ears.

"What's wrong?" Penelope asked.

"Mims has got a hunch we're walking into some kind of a trap."

"How could that be? They're all back there."

"Are they?"

A faint breeze stirred across the bunch grass levels, but it brought with it none of the canyon's smoke, for that was all to the east of us now. The clouds were heavy and it was now full dark. A horse stamped impatiently. The horses wanted water, they wanted rest, and they wanted grass. I had a feeling it would be hours before they were that lucky.

"All right," I said, "let's go on."

Moving ahead, I walked the dun slowly, pausing often to listen, but there was no sound beyond those to be expected—the sound of the horses' hoofs in the grass, the creak of saddle leather.

We were within two hundred yards of the Cienequilla when I drew up again, but again I heard no sound.

Flinch would have been the one on the mountain, of course, whether it was their idea or his. He would have been Indian enough to go up on the Rabbit Ears where he could watch everything that took place. He could not have seen us get the gold, but he could draw some conclusions from the way the pack horses moved.

So what would they do now? Wait in hiding until we had the gold out and loaded again? That would be what Bishop would want, but would the others be patient enough for that?

Suddenly I knew what I was going to do.

THIRTEEN

"Harry, do you know the peak called Sierra Grande? Due west from here?"

"I know it."

"Six or seven miles south of it there's an outcropping of lava and there's a peak there about four hundred feet high. When we get the gold loaded, you and Pen head due west for that lava flow and hole up somewhere south of the peak.

"You can water your horses on the Middle Fork of the Burro, but water won't be a problem. There are scattered ponds all over that country. Go on to the Carrizo if you want to, but it's about thirty miles, probably nearer forty the way you'll have to go to the peak. I wouldn't go out of my way if I can help it."

"What about you?" Penelope asked.

"It's dark. You move off quietly and they'll never know. I'll stay behind and tumble rocks around, cave in the bank here and there, make them think we were digging or hunting for the place. I figure I can give you an hour's start before they close in."

"And after they close in?"

"Why, there's liable to be a little difficulty, Penelope. I sort of doubt if they'll take my word, but I figure to be convincing."

"And then?"

"I'll come and join you."

There was a long moment of silence, and then she said, "There will be six of them—seven counting Sylvie... and just you."

"Maybe I can slip away before they close in."

"Why are you doing this?"

"That's a lot of gold."

"Wouldn't it be easier just to shoot Mr. Mims and me? There's only two of us."

"We're wastin' time talking like this. Anyway, I was never

101

much on doing things the easy way. We'll ride in now. If we're lucky we'll get the gold loaded and you out of here before there's trouble."

With that, I turned my horse and rode on to the creek. I felt pretty sure that they were close by, and that they would wait until we had the gold uncovered...it all depended on that. But you couldn't be sure about Sylvie and Ralph. Nobody knew when they'd go off half-cocked.

We dug the sand away with our hands, loaded the pack horses, with me counting the ingots as I had when we hid them. When they were all on the pack saddles I pushed Mims's shoulder as a signal for him to go.

Then, loud enough so a listener might hear if close enough, I said, "I tell you it was further this way!"

"You try it," Harry said, catching the drift. "I'll look down the creek."

Penelope had stopped beside me, and I turned and, putting my lips close to her ear, whispered: "Go on! I'll need every minute!"

She turned her head then and kissed me quickly on the lips, and I was surprised as if she'd stuck a knife into me...which I was half expecting.

Then she was gone.

Reaching up, I caught hold of a rock stuck in the sand at the top of the low bank, tugged it loose, and let it fall with a little cascade of sand.

"Ssh!" I hissed. "You want to start the whole country moving?"

Then I fumbled around in the dark, managed to step on a dried branch, to tumble some more dirt, and with a piece of the broken branch I dug at the dirt.

"Over further," I said. "It was over the other side about ten feet."

The minutes dragged. All of a sudden I knew myself for a damned fool. This wasn't going to fool anybody anywhere near long enough. My eyes went to the dun.

The horse was standing there, ground-hitched. One quick jump and I'd be in the saddle and riding out of here. How much was money worth, anyway? A man's life? Particularly when it was my life?

Suddenly, I heard a faint stir of movement on the far bank. Without waiting, I moved toward my horse. There was that movement again. After all, I had no friends over there. I palmed my six-shooter and let drive a shot right at the sound. Then I dropped to the sand, scuttled quickly five or six feet and came up running as two guns crossed their fire toward the point I'd just left.

There came a sudden crackle of flame and the brush across the creek exploded. Somebody had dropped a match into a dead juniper. The flames soared high, and the area was brightly lit. Instantly I heard the hard bark of pistols, the sharper report of a rifle, and a spout of sand leaped in front of me. Just behind me something slapped the water sharply and, turning, I saw a leaping figure and fired.

The man, whoever he was, caught in mid-jump, jerked oddly, and fell. He started to get up, then rolled off the bank into the shallow water.

Something seemed to tug at my sleeve, and then I was running, falling, running again. Another tree burst into flame ahead of me, and just beyond it I saw my horse.

Starting up the sloping bank from what was evidently a ford on the stream, I saw Ferrara. He had a rifle and was taking aim, not more than sixty feet away. My six-shooter was in my hand, and I simply fired, threw myself to one side, and fired again. He went down, tried to bring the gun around, but I had ducked from sight and was back in the stream bed running for my horse. Crawling up the bank, I grabbed the reins and jumped for the saddle, mounting without touching a stirrup.

The dun, not liking either the flames or the shooting, took off at a dead run. Behind me there were a few wasted shots, and then silence.

Riding north, I headed for the breaks along the North Canadian, knowing my first problem was to try to lead them away from Penelope and Mims, and the gold.

Also, I was going to have to find rest for my horse. Any wild mustang will travel for days, run a good part of the time, and get along on very little water, but carrying a rider is another thing.

After a brief run I slowed the dun, changed direction, and then reloaded my pistol and rifle. An hour or more later I holed up in a little hollow on a creek that fed into the North Canadian, stripped the gear from the dun, let him roll and then picketed him where he could reach the water. When I stretched out on the grass where I'd spread my blanket, I told myself I would not be able to sleep. A minute later I must have proved myself a liar, for when I awakened it was bright sunlight and I could hear the birds twittering in the willows.

For a long time, I lay still, looking up to where the sunlight fell through the leaves, and listening. There was a mag-pie fussing on a branch nearby, but after a few minutes he flew off. I sat up, put on my hat, shook out my boots, pulled them on, and stood up.

Slinging my gun belt around my hips, I buckled the belt, then walked over and talked to the dun for a while, all the time listening for whatever my ears could pick up. I tied my gun down with the rawhide thong around my leg, and went back and rolled up my blankets and ground sheet. Then I dug into my saddlebags for a busted box of cartridges and filled the empty loops in my belt.

I was hungry, but the little grub I'd had was used up, except for a little coffee, and I had no urge to hunt anything and draw attention by shooting. It wouldn't be the first morning I'd ridden off with no breakfast, nor would it be the last. I went to the creek and drank, watered the dun again, and saddled him up.

Riding west along the Corrumpaw Creek, I held to a line that would skirt Sierra Grande on the south. The clouds of the last few days were finally giving up some rain, which began to fall in a cold, steady shower, and I put on my slicker. From time to time I studied my back trail but saw nothing.

Had they gone off after Penelope and Mims, then? The two had a fair start, but with two heavily loaded pack horses they were not going to move very fast. However, Harry Mims was an old-timer, and a man who should know something about losing pursuit.

On the other hand, the hits I'd scored on two men might have cooled the others off somewhat. They could not know I was not with Penelope and Mims, or about to join them. I had no idea what the results of my shooting were. Both men were hit, and I hoped they were not killed, though wounded men are a sight more trouble than the dead.

That night, just before sundown, I sighted a sheep camp. There must have been over a thousand sheep in the lot, and three Mexican herders, with their dogs. The three were well-armed men, for this was Indian country, although we were getting closer to the settlements. I joined them, and soon learned that they were out of Las Vegas.

After I'd eaten I told them I was pushing on a ways. "No

reason for you to get into grief," I said. "There may be some men following me."

One of the Mexicans grinned slyly. "*Si, amigo*. Men have followed me also. *Vaya con Dios*."

Leaving them, I followed the south branch of the Corrumpaw until it lost itself in the steep slope of Sierra Grande, and made camp for the night. When daybreak came I found a bench and worked my way along it around the base of the mountain until the lava beds and their lone peak were due south of me.

The bench was five hundred feet or so above the land below and gave me a good view of the country toward the lava beds and the peak. Seated on a flat rock, I gave myself time to contemplate the country around that peak, which was a good five miles from where I sat. And that was a good mile south of the peak of Sierra Grande.

It was still early morning. Nothing moved down there. No dust clouds...nothing. When I'd watched for at least an hour, I mounted up again and let the dun find his own way down the mountain. We rode across the valley floor, raising as little dust as possible; after the light rain of the day before, that was no problem.

When I reached the lava beds I rode with caution, with my Winchester ready to hand.

There was nobody there...and no tracks.

Either they had never gotten here, or the tracks they'd left had been wiped out by the rain. For a while I scouted the country, and only once did I find anything like a track, and then it was only a slight indentation under the edge of a bush, such as a horse might have made in stepping past the bush.

Finally, I rode back to the peak. I'd told them to hole up somewhere south of the peak, so I tied my horse to a mesquite bush and climbed up on the lava.

I knew what lava would do to a pair of boots, and mine weren't in very good shape as it was. Scrambling around over lava, those boots could be done for in an hour or two, so I simply climbed the highest bulge I could find short of the peak and looked around.

The first thing I saw was an empty cartridge shell, bright in the sun. And a little beyond it, projecting from behind some brush, I sighted a boot and a spur.

It needed only a couple of minutes for me to get there. It was Harry Mims, and he was dead.

He had been shot in the back at fairly close range, but he was a tough old man with a lot of life in him and he had crawled—his scraped and bloodied hands showed that—trying to get away over the lava.

He must have lost his gun when they shot him. I didn't see it anywhere around and did not look for it. They had followed, caught up with him, and then standing over him had emptied a gun into his chest.

There were no other bodies, no horses, no gold, no Penelope.

Penelope?...A little chill caught me in the chest. Suppose she had killed him? Suppose it was she who'd shot him in the back, then followed him up and shot him in the chest to make sure of his death?

Who else could get that close?...And where was Penelope?

I left the place and rode to the west, cutting back and forth for sign. Almost a mile out I found where several horses, two of them heavily loaded, had crossed a wash, their heels sliding in the mud.

At intervals then I found sign; but I'd been following for scarcely another mile when in, glancing around to study my back trail, I thought I saw another trail off to the right. Riding over, I did find another trail—a lone rider keeping well off to one side, and often stopping beside a mesquite bush. Obviously, somebody had been scouting along the trail of the bunch of horses. I had no idea who the lone rider might be, but I knew Penelope had the horses, and I was sure there were no strange tracks among that lot.

Of the original group against us, I did not know which ones had survived, and were able to ride. Perhaps all of them.

It was just shy of noon when I found the other trail.

FOURTEEN

The new trail showed four riders coming in from the south, and a couple of the tracks were familiar ones. They belonged to some of the Bishop crowd. Who, then, was the lone rider following Penelope?

The trail held steadily west, then suddenly it ended in a maze of tracks. Drawing up, I stood in the stirrups and gave study to the ground.

The pursuers had lost Penelope's trail, and in trying to find it again had chopped up all the ground with hoof marks. Circling, I tried to pick up the trail of the lone rider again. From the way he had been acting I had an idea that he was a good tracker, and as he had been ahead of them, he was most likely to discover where Penelope had gone.

She had ridden into a belt of soft sand where tracks leave no clear impressions. Then she had evidently seen some herders coming with a flock of sheep and had simply ridden on ahead of them, keeping track of the direction they were taking and staying ahead so their tracks would wipe hers out.

The herd had been headed west, which was her direction, but I wasn't satisfied. She would not want to go north, for in that direction it was too far to any town where she could be sure of protection from the law. West was all right for her, but it was almost too obvious. Cimarron was over west, and she might head for there... but she might not. I found myself wishing I knew what she and Mims had talked about before he was killed. That old man knew this country and he had probably told her a good deal.

Those sheep were a good cover for her tracks, but it was likely Loomis, Bishop, and the rest of them would follow right along until they caught up with the sheep, and then they'd find her tracks. Yet I could not be sure of that. Suppose she turned off?

This girl was showing herself uncommonly smart. She was all alone now with three hundred pounds of gold, two pack horses, and a spare saddle horse, for she must have Mims's mount with her. She would outfigure everybody if she could, and I had a hunch she would leave that sheep herd at the first chance. She was, without doubt, riding a good way ahead of it. With that much gold she would be suspicious of everybody and taking no chance even with the herders.

So I held to the south edge of the herd, keeping an eye out for tracks. The herd was heading for a patch of junipers and piñon that lay ahead. There was good grass and a lot of good grazing on the slopes around those trees. A mile or more this side were twin peaks, with a low hill standing north of them.

When I got to that low hill I drew up and studied the ground. The sheep had passed north of it, but there were scattered tracks out from the flock, as there always are, and dog tracks among them. There was no sign of a horse track, but somehow I was not convinced.

Skirting the hill, I rode up between the two buttes that lay south of it. I'd been on the dodge too many times myself to ignore such a place. If she turned off between those buttes the sheepherders would have their view of her cut off until they passed the buttes, and by that time she could be under cover. They would not know which way she had gone.

On the far side of the buttes I suddenly came on several horse tracks, one of which I recognized. Yet I had gone on half a mile farther before I found more. She was using every bit of soft sand or hard rock she could find, and she left practically no signs.

Now the thing to figure was where she would be going. Cimarron was closest; if she by-passed that she could go through the mountains and turn north to Elizabethtown, or ride on to Taos. Each mile of this would be dangerous, but she had nerve, and evidently she had a plan. It was my hunch she would skip Cimarron.

Well now, here was a girl out of the East who was making fools out of the lot of us. One young girl, all alone, with four horses and three hundred pounds in gold, cutting across wild country toward . . . where?

Her trail was plain enough, so I lifted the dun into a canter and followed as rapidly as possible. She was hours ahead of me when she crossed the Canadian, but she was moving her pack horses too fast. Carrying a dead weight such as gold was harder than carrying a rider.

We were riding in cattle country now, and sooner or later she was sure to come up with some cowhands. Sure enough, she had, and did the smart thing. She swapped her horses for three fresh and better ones. But before she did the swapping she left her gold cached out in the hills.

She'd been gone less than an hour when I came into their camp. Right off, I noticed her horses in the remuda. They were beat, for they'd been ridden hard, and she had been smart to trade them off.

Me, I asked no questions at all. Like always, they invited me to set and eat, and whilst eating I made a swap for my dun. I was in no mind to let the dun go, and told them so, and they let me have a fresh horse that I could swap back for the dun at any time, they said. And that I meant to do.

"Ridin' far?" one of them asked.

I shrugged. "Yeah. Headin' to Mora to visit kinfolk. Name of Sackett."

"Heard of them." They looked at me with interest, for Tyrel and Orrin were known men in New Mexico.

The last thing I wanted those cowhands to know was that I was following Penelope Hume. They'd never tell me anything if they knew, for they'd all be on the side of a pretty girl, for which I'd not blame them.

"Seen a party of men north of here," I volunteered. "Look to be huntin' somebody."

The horse they traded me was a short-coupled black with some Morgan blood, and a good horse by any man's standards.

Riding out of their camp, I came upon the place where she had left the gold hidden while making her horse trade. She had loaded up, pack saddles and gold, and lit out as if the heel-flies were after her. Likely knowing she'd lost time, she wanted to get on with it.

Now I thought of Fort Union . . . she was headed for Fort Union. There were soldiers there, and she would be safe. The difficulty was that there would be a lot of questions asked about a young girl traveling across the country with all that gold.

But her tracks led right by the Fort, and by then I was actually within sight of her from time to time. I had no idea whether she had seen me, but if she had she knew she was headed for a show-down. I still wanted to know who had killed Harry Mims—shot in the back, at close range. Of the lone rider I had seen nothing in all this time. Nor had I seen anything of the others.

Suddenly I knew exactly where she was going. She was headed for Loma Parda.

The little town on the Mora River was rough and bloody, a resort for the soldiers at Fort Union, and for any number of drifters, male and female. They knew me at Loma Parda, but for her to ride into Loma with gold was like a lamb going to visit a lot of hungry wolves.

When she reached the town I was no more than four or five miles behind her, but there was simply nothing I could do. By the time I got to the town her horses were turned into a corral and Penelope had disappeared. It seemed the last person she wanted to see was me.

Avoiding the saloon, where I knew Penelope would not be, I went to a Mexican eating place down the street from Baca's. It was an off hour, and they were glad to see me. They knew me there, and the woman who came to wait on table shook her head when she saw me and said, "Señor Nolan, what do you do to yourself? You are tired!"

Glancing around, I saw myself in the mirror, a big, rough, bearded man who needed a shave, a bath, a haircut, and new clothes. He also needed about three nights of sleep.

"Señora," I said, "have you seen a girl—a girl with several horses?"

"Ah? It is a girl now? Si, I see her. She rode in today, only a little while ago."

"Where is she? Where did she go?"

"Go? Where can you go in Loma Parda? She did not go, she is here."

"Where?"

The señora shrugged. "Here . . . somewhere. How should I know?"

From where I sat I could look down the street and see anyone who moved, so I ordered a meal and stayed there, eating and drinking coffee and trying to stay awake.

There was not much out there in the street at this hour. In a little while the town would wake up, the soldiers would come in in one of the rigs that carried them over from the Fort, or they would hike, as many preferred to do. The town would be wide open. It was a town where killing was the order of the day, where the idea of gold would set the place afire. And somewhere in the town was Penelope, and three hundred pounds of gold.

Where did I fit in, anyway? I had given her a chance to get away, given Mims the same chance; but he was dead, murdered. And Penelope had not wasted any time looking for me, nor left any sign for me. And she had come here, to the least likely place. I couldn't even imagine her knowing of this place.

Rightfully, a piece of that gold was mine. I was the one who'd found it, I got it out of there, and now here I sat with about four dollars in my pocket and a nasty scar on my scalp to show for all I'd been through.

And then for the first time I remembered the money I'd been paid for guiding Loomis and Penelope. Fifty dollars...

I wasn't broke, then. Fifty dollars was nigh onto two months' pay for a cowhand, and I'd known a few who had worked for less.

While I sat there thinking about it, I saw Noble Bishop ride into the street. Jacob Loomis was with him, and Ralph and Sylvie Karnes. They come riding up the street, looking right and left, dusty and beat-looking, their eyes hot with the fire that only gold can light.

They did not see me sitting there, and if they went to the corral the big black horse would not be familiar to them.

But where was Penelope, and where was that gold?

And then I started to get really mad.

I'd been riding my fool head off, a good man had been killed and a couple of others less than good, and all for what? So one big-eyed girl could walk off with the lot, a girl with no more claim to it than any one of us. What if Nathan Hume was a relative? The gold had been buried for years, and without me she would never have had it.

I got up from the table so fast I almost upset it, dropped a half-dollar beside my place, and started for the door.

The señora ran after me. "Wait a minute, señor! Your change!"

"Keep it. Feed me sometime when I come in here broke."

It was hot outside in the late afternoon sun, but I did not care. I strode up the street and pushed open the bat-wing doors of Baca's saloon. Baca himself was standing at the bar, and I saw his eyes turn to me, narrowing slightly.

"Baca," I said abruptly, "there's a girl in town who came in this afternoon, and she's hiding out somewhere. You know everything that happens in this town—I want that girl, and I want her quick!"

"I am sorry. I—"

"Baca, I'm Nolan Sackett. You know me."

He hesitated. Within call he might have fifteen, twenty tough men. If he called them I was in for one hell of a fight. But right then I didn't care, and I think he realized it.

"She's down at Slanting Annie's. Not her crib—her cabin. You take your own chances. She's got a gun, and I hear she's ready to use it."

"She won't use it on me." But even as I said it, I wasn't sure.

I walked outside. The sun's glare hit my eyes like a fist, and I stood blinking. The anger was still in me, and I wanted only to see Penelope and know the truth. I had fought for her, helped her escape, found the gold for her—and then she had gone off on her own.

Mims was dead. Had she killed him? How else could anyone have come up on him? These thoughts went through my head, but in the back of my mind I didn't want to believe it.

Slanting Annie's cabin was under the cottonwoods on the edge of town. I walked down the dusty street, wishing I had a horse. No cowhand worthy of the name ever walked far on a street if he could avoid it, but there was no time to get a horse and the distance was short. All the time I knew that Bishop and the others were in town and would be hunting the girl, and me as well.

Annie herself came to the door. Slanting Annie had worked in a dozen western towns, and I had known her in both Fort Griffin and Dodge.

"Annie, I want to see Penelope Hume."

"She isn't here, Nolan."

"Annie," I said roughly, "you know better than to tell me something like that. I know she's here, and she'd better know that Loomis, Bishop, and all of them are in town."

"Let him come in," Penelope's voice said.

Annie stepped aside and I came into the shadowed room and removed my hat. Penelope was wearing a gray traveling outfit of some kind, and she was actually beautiful. I hadn't realized before just how beautiful she was, although I figured her for a mighty pretty girl.

"Mr. Sackett, I thought you were dead!"

"Like Mims, you mean?"

"Poor Uncle Harry...he never had a chance. Flinch did it."

"*Flinch?*"

Now, why hadn't I thought of him? There was Injun enough in him to be able to close in on a man without his knowing it.

"You expect me to believe that?" I said.

"Of course I do. You can't believe I would kill that fine old man!"

"You seem to manage pretty well when the chips are down." I dropped into a chair and put my hat on the floor beside it. "We've some talking to do."

She glanced at Annie. "Not now."

Annie looked at her, then at me. "You want me to leave so you can talk? You're perfectly safe with him," she added to Penelope.

I grinned at her. "Now that's a hell of a thing to say!"

"I mean that you're a gentleman. An outlaw, maybe, but a gentleman."

"Well...thanks."

"I'll go up the street. I want to see Jennie, anyway."

She took up her hat, pinned it on, and went out and closed the door.

"You're pretty good at getting across country," I said grudgingly. "That was a neat trick with the sheep."

"It didn't fool anybody."

"Yes, it did. It fooled them." I looked hard at her. "It didn't fool me."

"As for getting across country, I had a good teacher. Probably the best."

"Who?"

"Who else? You, of course. I watched you when you minded us, watched everything you did. You're a very careful man."

She was watching me with a curious expression that I couldn't quite figure out. "You haven't asked about the gold," she said.

"I was coming to that."

"I'm afraid you're not much of an outlaw, Mr. Sackett. I imagine a really successful outlaw would have asked about the gold first."

"Maybe."

I looked around the room. It was a small room in a small adobe house, but it was well furnished—there was nothing tawdry about it. I didn't know a lot about such things, but now and again I'd been in enough homes to know the difference between what was right and what wasn't.

"How'd you happen to know Annie?" I asked.

"Her aunt used to sew for my mother. I knew she was in Loma Parda, and I knew of no one else I could go to. I suppose you think a nice girl shouldn't even recognize Annie."

"I think nothing of the kind. Annie's all right. I've known her for quite a spell... in a manner of speaking.

"You know what would happen if anybody realized you had that gold? It would blow the lid off this town. And right at this moment they're hunting you."

"Annie knows a freighter. She was going to get him to help me get to Santa Fe." Then she said, "I had just made coffee— would you like some?"

While she went into the kitchen for the coffeepot and some cups, I sort of eased back in that plush chair. I didn't rightly trust the furniture. Benches and bunks or saloon chairs were more what I was used to, and I'm a big man. This sort of fine furniture didn't seem exactly made for my size. But it was a comfortable place and, looking around, I admired it. Even to the butt of the gun that showed from under a bit of sewing on the table.

Penelope returned with the coffee, poured some for me, and then seated herself, near the gun.

"The freighter was to leave tonight," she said. "He has ten wagons. Annie is arranging for me to have one of them."

"Where's the gold?"

She didn't answer that, but said, "I want you to have a share of it. After all, without you I might never have found it, and certainly I couldn't have kept it."

"Thanks," I said. "I can't set here waiting for them to come. I've got to find Loomis... and Flinch."

"Be careful of him. I had to run, you know. After Flinch killed Mr. Mims there was nothing for me to do. I was afraid of him."

I still held my coffee cup, but I was doing some fast thinking.

Not that I don't trust folks, but it began to seem to me she had been out of the room after that coffee just a mite longer than she should have been. I swallowed some coffee, put the cup down, and stood up.

"You're not going?"

"You'll be seeing me around. And when the time comes for that freighter to leave, I'll be back here."

Bending over, I picked up my hat. Her hand was near the gun—was that just accident? I took my time straightening up and saw she was looking at me, all bright-eyed. The trouble was, I wanted to trust her and almost believed that I could, but just wasn't able to gamble on it.

I went past her quickly and into the kitchen, opened the kitchen door, and stepped outside. On the small back porch I turned my eyes to the sun, and blinked a couple of times before stepping clear of the porch.

Back here there was a small stable, and the yard and the house were shaded by the cottonwoods. Somebody moved swiftly inside the house, and then I was at the front corner, looking across the street and up and down it. The first glance was swift, to locate any immediate danger, the second slower, carefully searching each possible hiding place.

It was a faint whisper of movement behind me that warned me. Turning sharply, I was in time to see Loomis lifting a shotgun. I palmed my gun and shot him through the middle, and both barrels of his shotgun emptied into the ground with a dull roar.

Instantly I was back under the cottonwoods and ran behind a long building, slowed down, and then walked out into the street to join a few others from the saloons.

"What happened?" somebody was asking.

"Shooting down the street," I said. "Maybe somebody killing a turkey."

I turned and walked up to Baca's, where things were stirring around. But there was no sign of Bishop.

The corral was my next stop. I got the black out, saddled him up, and left him tied outside the corral but well in the shadows.

A thought came to me, and I looked around the corral. Her horses were there, including the pack horses. But I saw no sign of the pack saddles. I had not been far behind her when she rode into town, and she must have known that. She could not have known where Slanting Annie lived, so she could not have taken the gold there. A young girl riding through Loma Parda's street with three horses, two of them pack horses, would have aroused interest, and this she would have guessed. So what then?

She would not have brought the gold to the corral, for she would have to unload it by herself, piece by piece . . . unless she just loosened the cinches and let the saddles fall. She could not have done that in town for fear of the packs bursting, or somebody seeing them and becoming curious at their weight.

So the gold must be somewhere out of town, quickly unloaded and left there before she rode in.

FIFTEEN

Standing with my hand on the saddle, I thought back along the trail. The sort of place she would need to hide the gold, where it could not accidentally be discovered, would be rare. Moreover, I had followed her trail in to Loma Parda, so how could she have veered off without my being aware of it?

Then I recalled that I had not actually followed her trail all the way into town. When her tracks merged with those of others coming or going, I had ceased to follow them and had merely taken it for granted that she was going on into town.

Stepping into the saddle, I skirted around the far side of the corral and rode down the alley toward the edge of town, and so out of sight of any watcher not in the stable itself.

There was another trail, I remembered, that led westward from Loma Parda toward the Sangre de Cristo Mountains, and then went south to Las Vegas and so on to Santa Fe. That trail was occasionally used by freighters, I knew. Supposing Penelope had skirted the town, come up close to that trail, and hidden the gold there?

In less than ten minutes I was riding along that trail, looking for possible hiding places. If I wanted to dump a heavy load, to be easily picked up again, where would I leave it?

It was still light, but the sun was down and it would soon be dark. My horse made no sound in the soft dust of the trail. But look as I would, I could find no place such as I sought.

Then at the last moment, with darkness closing around, I saw a patch of grass pressed down and almost yellow, some scattered pine needles and cones upon the grass. Drawing up, I studied the place. Something had been on that spot, something that was there no longer.

The mark, I saw, had clearly been made by a fallen pine tree,

a tree no more than ten feet high that had been blown down or
broken off and had rested there.

The tree was there, but it was now a few feet over to one side,
still fastened to the stump by a strip of wood and bark. Somebody
had picked up the top end of the tree and pulled it to one side,
leaving uncovered the place where it had originally fallen and
where it had been lying for at least several weeks.

Leading the black off the trail, I left it tied, and went over to
the tree. When I had pulled it aside I found the pack saddles, fully
loaded and not more than a few feet off the trail the freighters
would take. Each saddle held a hundred and fifty pounds of gold.

Reaching down, I caught hold of a loaded saddle with each
hand and straightened my knees. I walked off about fifty feet and
paused, resting the saddles, and then after a moment went on.
Twenty minutes or so later I returned and rode my horse all around
the area, trampling out all the tracks. Then I rode back into town
and tied my horse to the hitch rail in front of a store, now closed
for the night.

Carrying those three hundred pounds had been no trick for
me, for I'd grown up swinging a double-bitted axe, wrestling with
a crowd of brothers and cousins, and then going on to handling
freight on a river boat. After that I'd wrestled mean broncs and
thousand-pound longhorn steers. I guess I'd been born strong, and
anything I could pick up I could carry away . . . and often had.

But moving that gold would only help me for a matter of hours.
By daylight there'd be other folks hunting it. However, if a freighter
was pulling out with a train of wagons, I figured to be along. I'd
driven a team a good many times, and handled a jerk-line outfit
as well.

Standing in the darkness alongside my horse, I checked my
gun and my knives, for if ever a man was bucking for a fistful of
trouble it was me. If there were freighters about I figured they'd
be in Baca's saloon, and it was there I went.

The place was already half full of soldiers from the Fort, min-
gling with Baca's dance-hall girls, and he had him a plenty of them.
Here and there some tough-looking Mexicans stood around, and
they were Baca men, not to be taken lightly.

Baca's eyes found me as soon as I came in, and they watched
me as I worked my way through the crowd. When I stopped near
him I ordered a drink. "*Gracias,* Baca," I said. "I found her."

He shrugged. "*Bueno*. Annie tells me you are a good man."

"One thing, Baca. If any trouble starts around here, I want none with you. I've no argument with you, and want no trouble."

"*Si*, it is understood." He motioned for a glass and poured me a drink. "To you, señor, and good fortune." We drank, and then he placed his glass carefully on the bar. "Noble Bishop is in town. He was asking for you."

"I'm not trying to prove anything, Baca. If he wants me he's got to come asking."

"Is it about the señorita?"

Better for him to think that than to start wondering. "She's a pretty girl," I said, "and a lady."

"So I am told."

"Frankly," I said, "I'm hunting a job. Something to sort of keep me out of sight for a while. Riding or driving a freight team. But not a stage...nobody sees a freighter, but everybody sees a stage driver."

"There is a man in town—his name is Ollie Shaddock. He is taking some wagons out tonight, picking up more at Las Vegas."

I moved to a table near the wall, where I sat down and waited for Shaddock to come in. Most times I was a patient man, but now I was impatient, for gold makes a heavy weight on a man's thinking. It worried me that I had not seen Bishop, or Sylvie or any of that lot.

When Shaddock came in he was motioned to my table by Baca. I've no doubt Baca wanted to get shut of me.

Ollie Shaddock was a broad, cheerful man whose blond hair was turning gray. He thrust out a hand. "Anybody by the name of Sackett is a friend of mine. I'm from Tennessee, too."

"You know Tyrel and them?"

"I brought their ma and younger brothers west. I'm from the Cumberland."

"Me, I'm from Clinch Mountain."

"Good folks over there. I've some kin there. What can I do for you?"

"I want to hire on as a driver, or I'll drive for free. Only I want to be driving the last wagon when you pull out tonight."

His face sobered. "You tied up with that girl?"

"Sort of. I'll load what she thinks she's going to load. She'll get her share at Santa Fe...only I want to be sure I get mine."

"You're a Sackett. That's enough for me." He motioned for a bottle. "Nolan, I was the one who started Orrin in politics. In fact, it was because I was sheriffin' back in Tennessee that the boys come west.

"Tyrel, he wound up their feud with the Higginses by killin' Long Higgins. It was up to me to arrest him, and he went west to avoid trouble...me bein' a friend of the family, and all."*

"Well, can you leave me a space for a couple of loaded pack saddles in the middle of the wagon?"

"Sure enough." Shaddock filled his glass. "You know Tyrel and them?"

"No. Heard tell of them."

By now the place was going full blast and I wanted to get out; besides, I wanted to see if Penelope was all right. That girl worried me. I couldn't figure whether she was a-fixin' to get me killed or not. Maybe she'd been out in that kitchen pourin' coffee...but she might have been signaling Loomis.

Ollie Shaddock got up after a while and left, telling me where to meet them. It was sheer luck that he had turned out to be a friend of the family, and a man from the Tennessee hills. I'd heard of him before this, but only as being a man who operated several strings of freight wagons in New Mexico and Arizona.

After a few minutes I got up, paid what was asked, and eased out of a side door. Baca watched me go, no doubt glad to see me leaving. Not that fights were unusual in Loma Parda, for the town had been the scene of many a bloody battle, with many kinds of weapons.

The night was cool and still. Stars hung large in the dark sky, the cottonwoods rustled their leaves gently. I stood there, hearing the voices from inside and the tinpanny sound of the music from the music box. There was a smell of woodsmoke in the air.

I moved to the side of the door, where I waited, breathing easy of the night air and letting my eyes grow accustomed to the darkness. The last thing I wanted now was trouble. I had the gold hidden, I had a way of getting out of town, and in a matter of less than an hour we would be leaving.

When I moved, it was along the wall toward the street, and when I reached it I paused in the darkness looking both ways.

*The Daybreakers.

Down the street I could see a light in Slanting Annie's window, and I wanted to go that way. Annie would be at work by now, but Penelope would be there, waiting as I was.

She wouldn't be caring about seeing me, I knew, for I was no likely man to attract a girl's eye. Lifting my hands, I looked at them. Fit for handling guns or tools, fit for the hardest kind of work, for lifting the heaviest loads, but they'd found no call to gentleness, nor were they likely to. A girl as pretty as Penelope...

No use thinking about that. She had gone off and left me, leaving no sign. She might have murdered Harry Mims, and set a trap for me. Maybe it was like she said, that after he was killed she was afraid to be alone, but I couldn't trust her. The trouble was she looked so warm and friendly, so soft and lovely, that every once in a while my good sense went a-glimmering.

Somewhere around there was Sylvie and that brother of hers, and I'd given too little thought to Sylvie. But she'd probably given a lot of thought to me, and the chances were that she'd been working on Noble Bishop.

I stepped out on the street, which was partly lit by the light from the windows around, and walked toward the place where I'd left my horse.

The black nickered a mite and snuffed at my hand with delicate nostrils. I'd picked up a lump of brown sugar, and I fed it to him. Then I untied him and led him away into the darkness.

Well, it would soon be over. In a matter of minutes I'd be sitting up on the seat of a freight wagon, rolling out of town. Then I'd pick up the gold, put it aboard, cover it well, and we'd be rolling on toward Las Vegas and Santa Fe.

What would Penelope do when she found the gold gone? Would she come along, or would she stay behind and try to find it?

With these thoughts in mind, I mounted up and circled the town, working around to where the wagons were. Penelope should be there soon.

The wind was cool off the Sangre de Cristos, cool and fresh to the lungs, carrying the scent of pines and the memory of snows. Alongside the church I drew up and looked along the street. A wild Texas yell came to me from one of the saloons, then a shot... some celebrating soldier or cowhand. On the hills back of the town a coyote talked to the stars, complaining of something, by the sound of him.

When I reached the wagon I drew up alongside the last one and tied my horse to the tail-gate. I took my Winchester from the saddle boot and placed it behind the seat, but within easy grasp of my hand.

A man came down the line of wagons. "Sackett?" he said.

"Here."

He moved over beside me, his cigar glowing redly. "You set store by that girl?"

"Some."

"She ain't showed, and it's getting nigh to time. You think she'll back out?"

"Not likely." I considered. Was this another trap? She had told me she was going tonight. Was I now supposed to go looking for her? Or had Sylvie and Ralph finally caught up with her?

"How soon you want to go?" I asked.

"Fifteen minutes. I'm waiting for another wagon, loading over yonder."

"I'll go get her."

Ollie Shaddock said, "You better wait here. She wants to come, she will."

"I'll see."

"Sackett, I've heard talk around town. You better walk careful. Somebody has been hiring guns. You know how Loma is... you can get anything here you can pay for, and some things come cheap, like killings."

"Who's hiring?"

"No idea."

The wind off the mountains felt good on my face. It was no time for a man to die. Oddly enough, I was thinking less of that gold I would be picking up than of the wind in my face, or the girl. I had no meeting ground with gold. When it came to me I spent it and had little enough left to remember.

"Are you in love with that girl?" Ollie asked.

Was I? I didn't think so. I wasn't even sure I knew what love was, and I'd always guarded myself against any deep feeling for a girl. After all, who would want to live with me? I was a big tough man with two hard hands and a gun... that was me.

If it had been someone else I'd have answered with some

scoffing thing; but it was Ollie, and he knew people of my blood, and he was from Tennessee. "Ollie, I just don't know," I said. "I don't altogether trust her. The other one, that dark-eyed Sylvie, she's pure poison. Her I know. But Penelope? Well, I can't make up my mind."

"You step light, boy. Step light."

He meant it one way, but I decided to take it two ways, and I walked back to my horse and switched my boots for moccasins.

"Ollie, I'll be back. You just hold tight."

It wasn't more than a hundred and fifty yards to Annie's house, and I walked along under the edge of the cottonwoods. My mouth felt dry and my heart was beating heavy—I wasn't sure whether it was because I expected trouble or because of that girl. I told myself I'd no business feeling like that about any girl, but all the telling did no good, none at all.

I could hear music at Baca's; there men were singing and drinking and laughing, men playing cards and looking at girls and chinking coins or chips in their fingers. I could see the horses standing three-legged at the hitch rail, and I saw a man come from the walk in the darkness and cross toward Baca's, a man wearing a big sombrero, spurs jingling.

In the shadows under a big old tree I stood and looked at Slanting Annie's house. Lights in the windows, all cheerful and bright. Yet bright as they were, I felt an emptiness in me, a sudden longing for lighted windows of my own, and a coming home to them, opening the door to warmth and comfort and a woman waiting. Well, no use thinking of that, an unlikely thing for Nolan Sackett.

My moccasins made no slightest sound as I moved along under the trees. Long ago I'd learned to move like a wild animal in the wilderness. Boots would have made sound, but with the moccasins I could feel the branches under my feet before stepping down hard, and so shifted my step.

When I got to within fifty feet or so of the house I stopped again, holding myself close to the trunk of a cottonwood. There was no sound from within the house, and I moved closer and edged up to a window.

Penelope sat at the table, pouring coffee, and across the table from her sat Sylvie Karnes!

Shoulder to shoulder with Sylvie was Noble Bishop. Ralph

Karnes was coming in from the kitchen with a plate of cakes. Just as he put them down I heard Penelope say something about the time. All their heads turned toward the clock.

Penelope finished pouring coffee and sat back, taking up her own cup. There they sat, who were supposed to be enemies, talking together like at a tea party. I never saw the like. Maybe, after all, I was the only fool in the lot.

Then Penelope put down her cup, said something to Sylvie about the dishes, and went over and took up her bonnet. She turned and spoke to them all, obviously saying good-bye.

Like a ghost, I faded back into the trees and walked back quickly to the wagons. Ollie was waiting impatiently.

"She'll be along," I said.

"Did you talk to her?"

"No, but she's coming."

"She'll be in the wagon right ahead of you, since both of you wanted to stop."

"Who's driving hers?"

"A good man . . . Reinhardt. He's been with me a couple of years." Ollie looked around at me suddenly. "Never thought to tell you. Orrin Sackett is a partner in this outfit. He owns a third of it."

"He's done well, I guess."

"Yes, he has. I'd say he was one of the strongest political figures in the Territory."

Leaning against the wagon, waiting for Penelope to come, I reflected bitterly that Orrin had no more start than me when he came west. They had educated themselves, Tyrel and him, and both of them were big people in this country, while all I had behind me were a lot of dusty trails, barroom brawls, and lonely hide-outs in the hills.

The fact that I was about to pick up enough gold to make a man wealthy for life meant little when a body figured on it. What mattered was what a man made with his own hands, his own brains. Whatever I got out of this was from sheer chance and a fast gun. And right at this moment I didn't even have the gold.

She came walking up out of the darkness. "Oh, Mr. Shaddock, I'm sorry to be so late, but some friends dropped in and I just had to talk for a few minutes. Are you ready to leave?"

"Yes, ma'am. If you'll get up in your wagon, ma'am. This here is Oscar Reinhardt. He'll be your driver."

"Thank you." I could see her eyes straining toward me, a figure she could only dimly make out.

Ollie turned and gestured toward me. "Nolan Sackett will be driving the last wagon."

Ollie walked away toward the front of the train, and Penelope came back to me. "You're here then? I'm glad." She hesitated. "I'll have to admit that I'm glad to be leaving." Then she went on quickly. "I want to get away from this... this killing." She looked up at me. I could see the pale oval of her face in the darkness. "Poor Mr. Loomis was shot. He's not dead, but he was badly hurt. I can't imagine how it happened."

"This here is a dangerous country," I said. "Somebody might have seen him wandering around in the dark and figured he was hunting for them. I heard about the shooting. There were two shots fired, weren't there?"

"I don't know." She turned away from me and walked up to her wagon, where Reinhardt helped her in. After a few minutes I heard the first wagons moving out. As with all such freight outfits, they wouldn't really be moving as a unit until they were on the trail. Some of the wagons were standing off the side of the road, and they would be falling into place one by one. The movement would be a lot of stop-and-go until they finally got lined out. The stopping of a wagon would attract no attention for many of them would be stopped briefly while other wagons pulled in ahead of them.

Reinhardt's wagon moved out, and I let them get a start. I was driving a team of big Missouri mules, eight of them, and they handled nice. I'd always liked handling the straps on a good team.

We moved slowly while getting lined out, slower than a man could walk. I was watching for the marks I'd chosen and it was not many minutes after the wagons pulled out that I drew up. The wagon ahead was rolling on. I listened for a while, but there was no sound.

My hands wound the reins around the brake and I got down carefully, as quietly as possible.

Penelope might be in with Sylvie and them, but if she wasn't they would certainly be watching the wagon train move out. They would know that she had the gold, and that she must pick it up somewhere along the line. Would they be watching me too?

Climbing down the small bank off the road, I went into the trees, pausing from moment to moment to listen. I heard no sound that seemed out of place, and I stooped to pick up the pack saddles. Behind me I thought I heard a faint stir among the pine needles and junipers. Crouching, I listened, but heard nothing more.

I reached down into the hollow and lifted the first pack saddle out, then the second. I had been going to carry them both, but if I did I would be helpless if attacked. It was not so quick a thing to let go of such a weight and grab a gun.... One at a time then.

Picking up the first, I swung it to my shoulder and, keeping my free hand on my gun, walked back to the bank. There I needed the free hand to help me climb. I scrambled up and placed the pack saddle and its gold in the wagon, then went back for the second.

As I crouched by the second load, I listened again. I could hear the now distant, subdued sounds of the wagons—there was no special sound from Penelope's wagon. But I thought I heard something stirring up ahead. Taking up the second load, I lifted it to my shoulder and walked slowly and carefully to the bank. I put the gold down on the bank and, turning, looked all around, listening.

Nothing moved. Getting up on the roadbed quickly, I picked up the gold and lifted it into the wagon, then drew the tarpaulin over it and tied it in place.

I was standing beside the mules when I heard someone walking along the road. As he came up I saw that it was Reinhardt.

"Sackett? That girl's been out there ten minutes or more. What's this all about, d'you know?"

"I guess she had some packages she wanted picked up. Things look different in the dark and she's probably looking for them."

"Is that all?"

He was a good man, Ollie had said, and an honest man, no doubt. "Look," I said, "you better stay by your team. There's trouble in this, and there's no use in your getting shot over something that's no part of your business."

"Hell, I'm not afraid."

"Of course you're not, but that's not the point. You could get killed out there, and to no purpose."

"If that girl's in trouble—"

"Take it from me, she can handle it. Or I can. You sit tight."
One hand checked my gun. "I'll go get her."

I had no urge to go down into that black patch of juniper with
Penelope down there, and the Lord only knew how many others.
The smart thing to do was to stay right where I was and let her
get out under her own power.

All I would get down there was trouble. Nevertheless, that
girl was down there alone, and like a damned fool I went after her.

At this point there was no bank—the road was level with the
woods. Knee-high brush grew alongside the trail and I tried to step
over it to avoid sound, but I made a little.

First off, I headed for that broken-off tree where she'd had
the gold hidden. When I was almost there, something moved near
me, and I smelled a faint perfume.

"Penelope?"

A body moved against mine and a hand took my arm, a woman's fingers closing gently on my wrist. Suddenly those fingers
tightened and my wrist was jerked back, and at the same time I
felt her body move close to mine with a quick, violent movement.

My wide silver buckle that held my gun belt saved me, that
and my own reaction, for as the point of the knife hit the silver
and was deflected upward. My hand swept down in a blind, in-
stinctive action and struck her arm on the inside of the elbow.

Like I said, I'm a big man, and mighty strong, and that sudden
blow must have numbed her arm. She dropped the knife and I
heard it hit the ground. The next instant the whole place was lit
by a tremendous blaze of light. Somebody had dropped a match
into the top of that dead pine.

Now, anybody who has ever seen fire hit dead pine would
know what happened then. It went up in one tremendous burst
of crackling, spitting flame, lighting the entire area. And across the
space in front of me was Ralph Karnes, and not far away Noble
Bishop.

In the instant the light leaped up, Bishop saw me and I saw
him, and both of us knew the cards were on the table. His hand
dropped for his gun, and my instinct must have triggered my
muscles even before my brain realized the necessity, for my gun
sprang to my hand...a split second faster than his.

I felt the sharp whip of the bullet as it cut by my neck, and

I saw Bishop crumple and begin to fall. He caught himself with his left hand on a tree branch and started to bring his gun around on me. I shot into him again.

Karnes shot, but he was no gunfighter and he shot too quick. He must have pulled the trigger instead of squeezing, because he missed me. I didn't miss him. He backed up, clawing at his chest and spitting, then fell into the leaves, where he threshed around like a wild animal for a moment, then was still.

The brief burst of flame was dying down, and I looked around for Penelope. She was standing where the gold had been, almost as if unaware of all that had happened, just standing there saying over and over again, "It's gone... it's gone."

From the direction of town I could hear excited yells, and I saw a lantern bobbing in the distance as someone came toward us.

Without a word, I picked up Penelope and carried her to my wagon. "Get rolling!" I said to Reinhardt. "Try to catch up with the others. I'll take care of her."

"She all right?"

"Sure... now get going. I want to get out of here."

Reinhardt moved ahead and swung to his wagon. I put Penelope on the seat of mine, then climbed up beside her and took the reins from around the brake handle.

Reinhardt was moving out, and we followed. Mentally I counted my shots. Two bullets left in the pistol, no chance to load while driving the mules. The rifle was right behind me, within reach of my hand.

Suddenly, as the wagon began to move, Penelope came to life. "No, no! I can't go! The gold is back there! I've got to find it!"

"It isn't there," I said calmly. "It was moved within a short time after you hid it."

She turned on me. "How do you know that?"

"Relax," I said. "It's a long ride to Santa Fe."

"I don't want to go to Santa Fe! I want that gold!"

"They wanted it, too—Sylvie, Bishop, and them. Look what it got them."

Reinhardt's wagon had stopped again, then after a moment it started on.

"I need that gold," she said stubbornly. "I've got to have it. I don't know how to make a living, and there aren't any jobs for women."

"You could get married."

"When I marry I don't want it to be because I need someone to take care of me. I want to marry for love."

"Romantic," I said coolly.

"Well, I don't care—it's the way I feel!"

"You have all that gold, somebody would marry you because he wanted somebody to take care of him."

Reinhardt was sure doing an erratic job of driving. He had stopped again. I sat there, holding the lines, waiting for him to get going again.

"You couldn't find that gold now anyway. That place back there will be overrun with folks trying to figure out who shot who. If you figure to go back, you'd better wait a few weeks."

We drove on for a short distance, and then I said, "Did you have a nice talk with Sylvie last night?"

She turned sharply around on me. "You were spying!"

"Sure. A man has to know what's going on. I like to know who my friends are."

"And you don't think I'm your friend?"

"Are you?"

She was silent for a minute. Then she said, "I ought to be. You've done more for me than anyone else has. I don't think I'd even be alive but for you."

"You saved my bacon when I was down and hurt. You kept Ralph off me." I urged the mules a little faster. "And you did pretty well coming across the country alone."

"If you hadn't been coming somewhere behind me, I couldn't have done it. I knew you had to be back there, and I tried to do what you would have done."

"You did it well."

Neither of us said anything for a good while, just listening to the rumble of the wagon wheels on the road, watching the stars. But I was listening for other sounds too. By now my ears knew the sounds the wagon made, and the harness and the mules. I knew what sounds came from up ahead, and what the right night sounds were around me.

There was a missing piece somewhere.... Did Penelope have a knife ready for my ribs?

"That Sylvie," I said, "she tried to knife me."

"Where is she?"

"Back there. She may have a sore arm for a while, but she's going to live...worse luck."

"She's mean."

"I sort of gathered that. Sure as shootin', other folks will die because of her. I just hope we can stay shut of her."

That "we" sort of slipped in there, but Penelope didn't seem to notice it.

Then she said, "What could have happened to the gold?"

"Things look a lot different by night. You probably mistook the place."

"But that tree! I know it was under that dead pine!"

"There's lots of dead pines," I said carelessly.

"You certainly don't seem very upset about it."

"I'm not. I never had that much money in my life, so if I never see it again I ain't a-going to miss it."

We drove on, talking a bit from time to time, then she dropped off to sleep. It was daybreak when she sat up and began to push her hair into place and try to straighten her clothes.

"Where is the wagon train?" she asked. "We've fallen way behind."

"That Reinhardt! He's been taking it almighty slow. I didn't know until it got light that we were so far behind the rest of them."

Suddenly the wagon ahead pulled up. Nobody moved—the wagon just stood there. I got down and walked up to it. "Reinhardt," I said, "what's the matter? You gone to sleep?"

I looked into the muzzle of a gun, behind it the black, heavy-lidded eyes of Flinch.

"The belt," he said. "Unbuckle."

With this man I took no chances. Moving my hands with infinite care, I unbuckled the belt and let it fall to the trail.

"The bowie...take it out of the scabbard and drop it...fingertips only."

"Where is Reinhardt?"

Flinch jerked his head toward the wagon. "He is all right."

"How do you fit into this, Flinch? You working with Karnes?"

"I work for Flinch. My grandfather...he was in fight at Rabbit Ears. He was Indian. He tell me the white chief hide something there. A long time after he went back to look, but could not find. When I hear talk in Fort Griffin about Rabbit Ears, I get a job."

The way the wagons stood on the trail, Penelope could not see us. I heard her getting down from the wagon and heard the sound of her feet.

"You too," Flinch said as she came up. "You stand over there. Beside him."

For the first time his thin lips smiled. "Now, after all, the Indian gets the gold."

"The gold isn't here, Flinch," Penelope protested. "It's back there, at Loma Parda."

"The gold in his wagon." He nodded toward me. "I follow him. I know he will find it, so I follow, watch him when he hide it, watch him when he load it in wagon. It is better for me to have the wagon for a while... the gold is much heavy."

Penelope stared at me. "You had that gold all the time? You mean you had—"

"Now I am going to kill," Flinch said. "First you, then her."

"Let her take my horse and go."

He did not even reply. I took a half-step toward him. "Up!" he said. "*Manos arriba!*"

I lifted my hands as high as my ears. He kept his eyes on me, wanting to see the effect of his words. "I kill you. I keep her until tomorrow."

"They'll hang you," I said. "Look here, Flinch, let's—"

My right hand, only inches from my collar, moved suddenly. The knife slung down my back, slid into my hand, the hand whipped forward, and he fired. I felt the slam of his bullet, heard the thud of my knife. It had gone into the hollow at the base of his throat, up to the hilt.

His mouth opened in a great gasp and blood gushed from it. He fell forward to his knees, grasping at the hilt, fumbling to get hold of it with both hands, but I had thrown with all my strength and the knife had gone in hard.

He struggled, choked, then fell over on his side, the knife coming free in his hand.

Stooping down, I took the knife from his fingers and sank it twice into the sandy earth to cleanse the blade. Penelope was looking at him, her eyes filled with horror.

"See what happened to Reinhardt," I said sharply. "Be quick!"

Startled, she turned and hurried to the wagon. When I looked back at Flinch, he was dead.

Belting on my gun again, I stripped Flinch's gun belt and tossed it into the wagon.

Reinhardt came out from under the wagon cover, rubbing his wrists. "He wouldn't have killed me, I think," he said. "I staked him a couple of times when he was broke."

"We'd better move on. Ollie Shaddock will be wondering what happened."

He glanced at me, then at the dead man. "What happened? He was sure enough going to kill you."

I reached back and drew the knife again. "This," I said. "I learned it south of the border."

I started back to the wagon. Penelope joined me, and I helped her up. Reinhardt was already moving off.

We had been traveling for some time when she said, "You had the gold all the time!"

"Uh-huh."

"What are you going to do with it?"

"Been contemplating on that. Likely I'll give half of it to you."

"You'll *give*—!"

"And I'll keep the other half myself. That way," I continued, "you'll be free to marry for love. But with half of that gold, I won't need anybody to take care of me, either, so you won't be married for what you have."

She didn't say anything to that, and I didn't figure she needed to, the way things were shaping up.

"I thought you got hit back there," she said presently.

So I showed her where the bullet had hit my cartridge belt right on my left hip. It had struck the lead noses of two bullets, fusing them into one. "I'll have a bad bruise, the way it feels, but I'm the luckiest man alive."

Only thing was, I surely wished I had a shave. And before we got to Santa Fe she was wishing it, too.

AUTHOR'S NOTE

Borregos Plaza was on the south bank of the Canadian River, only a short distance from the river crossing tat was to become Tascosa. Tascosa went from a booming and untamed cow town to a ghost town, and is presently the site of Boys' Ranch, founded by Panhandle businessmen.

Romero, a small town in ranching country, has a long memory of buffalo hunting and Indian fighting days. The country around is little changed from the period of my story.

The Rabbit Ears, known to many travelers along the Old Santa Fe Trail, is only a little way from the town of Clayton, New Mexico. The box canyon featured in the story is there, so is the pool, which is usually covered with a green scum, and there is also an open hole some three to four feet in diameter. Around it the walls and rocks are blackened by fire, likely the result of some explosion of oil or gas.

Loma Parda on the Mora River is now a ghost town, some eight miles northwest of Watrous, New Mexico. When Fort Union was abandoned the town began to die, but in the 1870's it had a rough and bloody reputation.

At the time of my story the buffalo hunters still had two or three good years ahead of them, and they would be replaced by cattlemen. Practically the only settlers in the Panhandle country then were Mexicans from Taos or Mora with their sheep.

The Sostenes l'Archeveque mentioned early in the story was a notorious outlaw and killer of the period, often credited with twenty-three killings. He was killed by his own people when his conduct became too unruly.